Be love Lily Harlem

EMBRACED BY THE EMPEROR

Hawk Castle, Book 3
A Habsburg Historical Romance

by Lily Harlem

"What Mars gives to others,
Venus delivers to Vienna."

DRAGONBLADE PUBLISHING, INC.

ARE YOU SIGNED UP FOR DRAGONBLADE'S BLOG?

You'll get the latest news and information on exclusive giveaways, exclusive excerpts, coming releases, sales, free books, cover reveals and more.

Check out our complete list of authors, too!

No spam, no junk. That's a promise!

Sign Up Here

www.dragonbladepublishing.com

⫸⫷

Dearest Reader;

Thank you for your support of a small press. At Dragonblade Publishing, we strive to bring you the highest quality Historical Romance from some of the best authors in the business. Without your support, there is no 'us', so we sincerely hope you adore these stories and find some new favorite authors along the way.

Happy Reading!

CEO, Dragonblade Publishing

Additional Dragonblade books by Author Lily Harlem

Hawk Castle Series
Loved by the Last Knight (Book 1)
Adored by the Archduke (Book 2)
Embraced by the Emperor (Book 3)

The Lyon's Den Series
Lyon at the Altar

Embraced by the Emperor

When your destiny is tied to just one man, should you wait in hope, join a convent, or start fighting for what you know is rightfully yours?

Isabella of Portugal has two choices: to wed the handsome and powerful Holy Roman Emperor, Charles V, or don a habit and betroth herself to God.

Unfortunately, her potential future husband is flitting around Europe doing what emperors do and he seems to have forgotten a wife and heir are needed.

Until, that is, he finally sees sense and travels to Seville to claim his bride.

From that moment on, Charles's life is never the same. Isabella is captivating, intelligent, and a political force to be reckoned with. He is as smitten as he is in awe.

But the sixteenth century is a time of turbulence and unease, battles and deceit. With Henry VIII wreaking havoc with Rome and King Francis a thorn in the emperor's side, can he keep his empress happy and safe? And will they get their longed-for fairy tale ending?

Notes from the Author

While writing HAWK CASTLE, I have truly let my imagination run wild and free to create a fun, romantic romp through history in the company of an eclectic bunch of vibrant, powerful, and passionate men and women.

In other words, while this story is inspired by long-ago characters and events, please don't quote HAWK CASTLE in your history thesis, as I can't be responsible for your grade!

By the way…

*By the fifteenth century, the Habsburg family had become the most powerful family dynasty of all time. Their lands were so expansive and covered such vast swaths of the globe that it was said 'the sun never set on the empire.'

**Habsburg Archduke Charles of Austria was first elected Holy Roman Emperor in 1519 after his grandfather Maximilian I died. He was then crowned Elected Holy Roman Emperor in 1520, then again crowned as Holy Roman Emperor by Pope Clement in 1530. He was Holy Roman Emperor from 1519, but the last crowning, conducted by the pope, meant the title was hereditary to the Habsburg family.

***Big families were the norm back then, but Charles's brother, Ferdinand, had fifteen children with his wife, Anna of Bohemia and Hungary. Quite something when it is said on his wedding night he was so clueless, he had to have instructions given from the bedside. I guess he got the hang of it!

PROLOGUE

1522
England

"YOU WANT ME to…let me be clear I understand correctly… you want me to become betrothed to Mary? To wed her?" Charles stared at Henry, King of England, and had to stop his mouth from dropping open at the absurd suggestion. "Your…Your daughter, Mary?"

"Emperor, I am sure your young ears work perfectly well." Henry crossed his arms, bunching his ermine-lined royal robe of crimson and gold, and sat back on his large, golden chair. "My wife and I believe it is the perfect solution. An auspicious melding of our families and nations and a way to ensure future negotiations are peaceful. Your parents visited here, you know, after they were…shipwrecked, for want of a better word. Stayed quite a while with my father, charmed he was by them both."

"Mmm, yes, I have heard the story." Charles resisted a deep frown and looked at his aunt for assistance.

Catherine, Queen of England, merely took a sip of wine then raised her right eyebrow at him in a way that reminded him of his mother when she'd been expecting better of him as a young boy.

He took a deep breath and set his hands on the table, fingers spread wide. Sunlight from the warm, June day sliced through the high window to reflect off his heavy signet ring. "But she, Mary, your daughter, is but four years old."

"That is correct," Henry said with a sharp nod.

"I will wait half my life before I am married."

"Nonsense." Henry chuckled and fiddled with his necklace. The diamond suspended from it was the size of a walnut. "Ten years is all and then you shall wed. I am sure God has given you patience in your royal blood."

Charles felt his jaw tense. If anyone other than Henry had spoken to him this way, he'd slam his fist onto the table and order them gone from the room. But right now, he was in Henry's Windsor Castle and being Holy Roman Emperor would only go so far in getting him out of there alive should he anger the king. Congenial he might have been on the surface, but there was an undercurrent of menace.

"I agree," Charles said, trying to sound diplomatic, "the marriage would strengthen our countries' bonds, but right now, France is our problem, not whom I marry. You have just declared war upon King Francis, remember."

Henry held up one hand, a mass of bejeweled rings, and waved dismissively. "Of course I remember, and Francis will learn a hard lesson, one that ensures he pays me my dues and then regrets his latest invasions." He leaned forward suddenly, urgently, and clasped his hand over Charles's. "Do you forget so quickly the *Henry Grace à Dieu*, the greatest warship the world has ever seen and that is now on your side, Emperor? At your disposal…should I wish it to be."

"I remember. It is a very fine vessel." He'd been impressed by the warship. The shining hull was colossal. The masts towered into the sky and the rows of cannons staring from their holes were particularly menacing. And it was just the first in Henry's imposing armada.

"And," Henry went on, "do you forget how we marched as one, as brothers in arms, into London just last week to a lavish festival of music, banquets and jousting? The streets were lined with triumphant arches, tapestries, and pageants. The English people adore you,

Charles."

Charles tilted his chin, then rubbed the small, vertical dent at its center. He was freshly shaven and his skin satisfyingly smooth. "You do know that when I was a child, my father negotiated my marriage to King Louis of France's daughter?"

"Yes, I am aware, and I believe Isabella of Portugal is the latest to have been mentioned." Henry studied him, his small, intelligent eyes searching. "She would make a rich wife for you. An empress of fine, pious standing."

"Yes." Charles nodded slowly, determined not to be cowed by Henry's intense scrutiny or manipulated by him even one tiny bit. "That is a truth."

"But don't you see?" Catherine said in a slow and steady voice. "With such uncertainty in the empire, you need this alliance with England. You may be my nephew, and very dear to me, but I will not be able to protect you and your lands without this promise of marriage to Mary. To our Mary."

"Who will be the most suitable empress of them all and be eternally by your side." Henry nodded slowly. "She is your destiny."

Charles bristled but again tried not to show it. He was a powerful man, with great lineage and a sharp insight into politics. But he was also wise enough to know he could not control everything all of the time. To think otherwise would be dangerous. For now at least, he'd have to agree to this suggestion of marriage.

"I understand," he said, holding in a sigh as he thought of the letter he'd have to write to Isabella of Portugal. A woman he'd never met but one he had promised to marry soon after his ascension to the Spanish thrones of Castile and Aragon. "And right now," Charles went on, "France is a bigger threat than the Ottomans, so yes, I will agree to marry Mary in due course in order to bind our countries together."

"Very good." Henry sat back and clapped. "We will drink to celebrate."

"On one condition…" Charles held up his hand and narrowed his eyes.

"Go on?" Henry appeared surprised there would be a condition. How very vain he was.

"She must be at least eighteen."

Henry's lips pursed.

"I will not wed a child," Charles said.

Henry sighed, then he nodded. "I can agree to that."

"And in the meantime, do not expect me to be a man without lovers and, perhaps, children." Charles raised his eyebrows. "I am not a monk and do not wish to live as one."

"They will be nothing. They will be illegitimate children," Catherine said firmly. "Born out of wedlock and with no claims to any titles or lands. They will mean nothing."

Charles was thoughtful. If he had illegitimate children in his future, which was a distinct possibility with fourteen years to wait until marriage, he would ensure he had their loyalty and respect and that they knew exactly who their father was. Delegation was going to be key going forward with imperial business and whose better loyalty than family's? "These children, dear Aunt, at present are a hypothetical problem," he said with a dismissive shrug. "So let us have that drink and toast to a Habsburg and Tudor union."

"To our union." Henry reached for his wine, picking it up swiftly and causing it to slosh a drip of deep claret onto his hand. "And defeating France. Let us also toast to the downfall of Francis, the conniving snake that he is."

>>>———<<<

ISABELLA STARED OUT of the window at the trees swaying in the brisk, Atlantic breeze. Autumn was on the way and the first leaves were skittering through the air. Still, it never got too cold in Lisbon, nothing a good fire and a warm cloak couldn't cure. She'd heard the winters were harsh in the Low Countries, where her betrothed, the Habsburg Archduke Charles, had spent his childhood. Perhaps when they were wed, she'd travel there with him, in which case she'd needed warmer gowns, fur capes, and velvet headwear.

The sharp click of footsteps on the hard floor made her turn.

"John," she said when she saw her brother's tall, lean frame striding toward her.

His boots were polished, his tunic emblazoned with the red and gold shield of the family crest, and his black beret sat at a slight angle. He wore a silken, scarlet cape.

"I thought you had gone hunting for the day," she said.

"I was just about to." He held up a scroll. "But this arrived by envoy."

She raised her eyebrows. It was unusual for the King of Portugal to tell her about an envoy delivery. He had so many, his interests spreading far and wide across the globe. "May I ask whom it is from?"

He didn't even glance at the seal; it was clear he already knew. "The Holy Roman Emperor."

"Charles." She instinctively reached for the cross her mother had left her that now sat around her neck. "It has been some time since we heard from him. Perhaps he is keen for us to set a date for our wedding ceremony. I would be most glad if he is."

"It is true, you are of age now." The king nodded seriously then walked to a heavy, wooden table before an unlit fire and broke the seal on the scroll. "My only fear is the dowry I offered is not enough, and that he requests too high a price."

She gathered the hem of her blue, silk gown and rushed to him. "Whatever the price, we must pay it, brother." She rested her hand on his arm. "I implore you."

He studied her. "And if it is a sum we do not have?"

"We will raise it. It is my destiny to marry the emperor. It is what mother decreed in her will."

His heavy eyebrows pulled together. "It was her wish that you marry a *king* or *become a nun*, if I remember correctly."

"I wish neither to marry a king nor to be a nun." A rush of determination flooded her and she tilted her chin. "I wish to marry an emperor." She raised her eyes heavenward. "That would please our mother even more, God bless her soul."

"It is true, it would please her. Charles is the greatest king of Christian Europe we have ever known."

"And together, we could continue our grandparents' ambition to unite all the good and pious Christian countries." Isabella was warming to her subject. "The fight against the Ottomans is real. Why they dare to advance on our doorstep and—"

"You do not need to tell me of the dangers Sultan Suleiman poses. His capture of Belgrade is proof enough." John's cheeks flushed, as though angered just at the memory.

"Brother. Dearest brother. You must promise me before this scroll is read that you will do everything in your power to make me empress."

He sighed, then leaned forward and kissed her brow. "Your happiness is of great import to me. I wish you to know love as I have."

Her heart squeezed. "I know how you wished to marry Eleanor. I am so sorry."

"That is in the past." A flash of sadness crossed his eyes. "Let us not talk of lost love."

With a flourish, he unfurled the scroll.

The emperor's crest shone from the top of the letter then beneath it black ink flowed in neat loops and lines across the page.

King John, dearest cousin and most illustrious monarch of Portugal,

I, Charles, Holy Roman Emperor, King of Spain, Archduke of Austria, and Lord of the Netherlands write to you this day on matters of much import for both of our empires.

It is my wish that you marry at the earliest date my youngest sister, Catherine. This union of the pious Iberian states of Spain and Portugal would please me very much and I am confident in your positive response.

And with this union comes a change in my plans with your sister Isabella.

I am now betrothed to Mary Tudor, daughter of Henry VIII King of England and his queen, Catherine of Aragon. This marriage will, I am sure you will agree, secure the Iberian Peninsula's future good relations with England during this fractious time with France and the threat of the infidels from the East.

Charles V

"Oh, dear Lord, have mercy on me." Isabella's eyes filled with sharp tears. "He is to wed Mary of England...but...oh...John." She shook her head, hardly able to believe what was happening. "She is but an infant princess. How could he? I...I don't understand."

John snatched up the scroll and screwed it into a tight ball with both hands. He then threw it at the unlit fire, where it bounced and rolled onto the hearthrug. "Of all the..."

"Oh..." Isabella felt quite faint, disappointment a brittle band around her chest. "This is so upsetting." She staggered to a chair and sat, found a kerchief, and dabbed at her cheeks.

"Of all the scheming, lying, manipulative..." John stomped to the window and stared out with his hands on his hips, his cape flowing over his angled elbows. "He still dares to think he can order me whom I can and cannot marry."

"And breaks an engagement with me," Isabella said as her dreams fluttered away like moths after a lantern extinguished. "After all of these years of waiting, I get not even a letter to me personally or..." She held in a sob. "An apology."

"Charles is too big for the boots he wears," John said sharply. "His self-import has no bounds or decency."

She studied his broad shoulders. "What will you do?"

"He knew full well it was his elder sister, Eleanor, I wished to marry." He turned and pressed his hand to his chest, over his heart. "Yet he refused that request and now offers Catherine, a woman of whom I know nothing and who is much younger than Eleanor."

Isabella kissed her cross again and sent a silent prayer to God, asking him for strength. "I am sure Catherine will make a good wife."

"That is not the point." John threw up his hands. "He denies my heart and snubs you. I should break all relations with Spain. In fact, the devil in me wishes to side with Francis and take out my frustration with an army. That would teach the emperor a lesson he wouldn't forget."

"That may be so." Isabella tucked away her kerchief and reached for a goblet of wine. "But my namesake would turn in her grave if we were to do such a thing. She hated France."

John sighed. "I know you are right. The Queen of Castile would want this union. She always supported Spanish and Portuguese marriages."

"Our grandmother was a prudent woman." In that moment, Isabella had a sudden swell of determination. It was as if all the tales her mother, Maria, had told of her grandmother blustered into her memory at once. Queen Isabella of Castile had been a strong, intelligent, and patient woman. Her faith had been unwavering and her standards exceptionally high.

And that very same blood ran in Isabella's veins on this day. She, too, would be strong and patient. She, too, would have faith and not let go of her dreams. "I *will* marry him," she said, standing and enjoying the rush of energy that came to her limbs. "Perhaps not this week or this year, but the emperor will see that being betrothed to an infant is not the course his life should take. He needs a woman who is educated and multi-lingual, one who has a keen mind for politics."

John studied her. "I fear Charles will not deny the King of England now this pact has been made."

"He will." Isabella took a sip of wine. "For what hot-blooded man with ambitions beyond our imaginings will wait many years to sire heirs?"

John was quiet for a moment, then, "It is true. He must be impatient to secure his successor."

"And continue the Habsburg bloodline. What better way to do that than with me? I will give him sons of pure blood. It is I"—she tapped her chest—"who will fulfill his destiny and dreams."

John walked up to her and gently touched her cheek. "I see our mother in you when you speak this way."

"It is true she was indomitable, but know this: I am determined in this outcome and also wise. I know I must be patient, as an emperor cannot be told what to do. He will come to me when his own mind reaches the conclusion that it is I, Princess Isabella of Portugal, who should be the empress on the throne at his side."

"And if you don't become his wife? If he never reaches this conclusion? You will become a nun?"

"Yes. I will wait until my childbearing years are over, and at that point, I will devote myself to the Holy Father. But know this, dear brother, before you have thoughts of marrying me off for political gain: Charles is the only man with whom I will stand at the altar, the only husband to whom I will declare my faithful obedience before God. Any other, and I will drink poison the night before my wedding."

CHAPTER ONE

1525

Pavia, Northern Italy

CHARLES SAT ASTRIDE his warhorse and stared through the dawn mist at the violent, bloody scene unfolding before him.

The town of Pavia had been under siege by King Francis of France for the entire winter, but now the time had come to fight back.

And fighting was what Charles's landsknechts—savage mercenaries from Germany—did best. With pikes, hammers, swords, and daggers, they steamed through the French infantry with the imperialist flags flapping wildly above them and their swords slashing and pikes stabbing.

Lannoy, Viceroy of Naples and Charles's military commander, urged his horse forward. "Be careful, Your Majesty," he shouted over his shoulder to Charles. "The landsknechts are ruthless killers. And they have been known to switch sides mid-battle if the other offers more gold."

"They have been well paid. They will be loyal to their emperor," Charles shouted. In truth, he only had enough money to pay them for a few more days, which was why he'd had no choice but to come up with a plan.

He'd ordered engineers to break through the fortified walls surrounding Pavia so that his men and the landsknechts, plus Spanish and Neapolitan soldiers, could break out with surprise on their side, and attack Francis's armies dotted around the vast park.

It was reported King Francis himself was close by, perhaps in nearby Mirabello Castle.

Alfonso, sat astride a huge, black horse with yellow and red feathers rising from its armor, pressed his steed forward. "Your grandfather has a lot to answer for, Your Majesty, since it was he who created this landsknecht army for sale. It is said that even the devil himself won't let them into hell because he is so afraid of them and—"

A rattle of field guns rushed forward, clattering and banging, instructions being shouted to the men dragging them through the mud. Alongside, soldiers with long guns marched into the fog.

"I will take the guns and arquebusiers south so we can attack on the left flank," Alfonso called over the din. "God be with you."

"And with you." Charles commanded his horse on, keeping pace with Lannoy.

Overhead, the sun, a dusky, white orb, barely penetrated the dawn haze. With each step, a new scene of battle unfolded in Charles's vision. "I believe we have driven a wedge between the two French camps."

"Yes, Your Majesty, in only a few hours." Lannoy broke into a canter. "We should make for Mirabello Castle and see if the king is still holed up there."

Charles followed Lannoy, his horse jumping over a dead body and then a ditch with a macabre bloody stream running through it. His own body was alive with the fight. He was a skilled warrior. And now, with the scent of victory in the air, it was hard not to be excited. Oh, how he'd enjoy the look on Francis's face when he learned that his troops had been defeated and his plan to take Pavia and beyond had been foiled.

As they moved past the woodland and irrigation ditches, it was clear his soldiers had the upper hand all around them. Charles urged his horse faster and then a cluster of French troops in plumed helmets and full plate armor, set in four ranks, came into view. Heavy lances at the front, then lighter lances, swords, spears, maces, and finally, the archers at the back.

"They are well-armed," Charles shouted to Lannoy, "and include Black Band defectors."

"Yes, but our troops are fresh and there are many more of us. And Alfonso has blocked their assistance. They are on their own."

Charles drew to a halt. "We should charge."

Lannoy also stopped, his horse pawing the floor and snorting. "Yes, but, Your Majesty, you must wait here."

"No, I will fight my fight." He banged his fist against his armored chest.

"I beg of you not to. You are emperor and I cannot let it be my legacy that I allowed you to fight to your death."

"I cannot ask men to do something I am not prepared to do," Charles shouted.

"These men are paid to fight and die—they are doing their jobs. Your job is to rule, to unite Christendom. Please. Wait here. I implore you."

Much as it irked Charles because he was itching to wield his sword against the brazen French, he knew his commander was right.

"Good," Lannoy said, taking Charles's silence as agreement. He turned to the infantrymen and raised his right hand. "There is no hope left except in God. Men, follow me and do as I do."

The roar of the charge rang in Charles's ears and he struggled to stop his horse from joining the stampede. He turned the creature in circles and weaved it this way and that, its hooves splashing in the soggy ground and its armor clanking.

Through the mist, cries of agony swirled and the clatter of metal on metal echoed. Horses free of their riders made for the treeline bloody and stumbling. Several French soldiers disappeared after them, retreating, fleeing.

It seemed as though the battle went on for hours, though in truth, Lannoy and the imperial landsknechts made quick work of the French troops, slaying them where they'd stood in formation.

"Your Majesty!" One of Lannoy's commanders appeared at Charles's side. He was missing the armor on his right arm and his bloodied hand clutched a dagger. "Lannoy…he…"

"He is dead?" Charles called.

"No, no… Come, this way… You must come with me…" The commander swung around and took off at a gallop.

Charles didn't hesitate. He took chase wondering what on Earth had happened for Lannoy to send for him when not long ago, he'd insisted he, as emperor, hold back.

He rode for only a hundred yards before he saw the chaos.

Lannoy's horse was rearing and plunging as Lannoy swung his sword violently through the air at a bunch of bloodthirsty soldiers. "I order you to back down! Back down, I say!"

"What is going on?" Charles asked, riding into the fray.

It was then he saw him.

King Francis.

A streak of blood slashed over the king's large nose and his cape was torn. His armored vest was mud-strewn and his sword baked in blood.

Charles drew to a swift halt at his side, sandwiching the king between himself, Lannoy, and the commander.

Francis stared up at Charles, his dark eyes flashing.

"Sire," Charles said, the full enormity of the situation dawning on him. "Are you severely wounded?"

"No, hardly at all," Francis said, gripping his sword hilt.

"Good, then that is how it shall remain." Charles removed his helmet, tucked it beneath his arm, and turned his attention to his angry mob of Spanish and Neapolitan soldiers.

"Arquebusiers," he shouted. "My countrymen, my brave soldiers, there will be no more death today, for there has been enough before the sun has even broken through the dawn clouds."

The shouting around him quieted and he made eye contact with as many men as he could. It wasn't hard, as they were all looking at him with admiration and curiosity, clearly surprised the Holy Roman Emperor had suddenly appeared on the battlefield.

"The King of France is among us, it is true," Charles shouted, "but we have succeeded in our mission and are victorious in not only freeing the town of Pavia from the winter-long siege but also in capturing the most prized prisoner of all." He looked down at Francis and raised his eyebrows. "One we must take alive, for that triples his value to us."

"Kill him. Kill him," someone shouted.

"No!" Charles spotted the heckler. "I order, as your emperor, that he be unharmed."

"Why shouldn't we kill him?" Another soldier with blood running from his temple shouted. "He is our enemy."

"Because wars are not just fought on the field with pikes and swords," Charles said. "They are also fought in chambers with words and politics, and it is the words and politics that will, from this point, bring peace and prosperity to all of Italy." He banged his hand on his chest. "I tell you this from my heart: The Italian wars that have caused so much suffering can go on no longer if I have the French king as my prisoner. Kill him here, now, and you will spawn another king, one who may regroup." He looked down at Francis again as the crowd quieted. His words were clearly resonating.

King Francis was staring up at Charles with a defiant set to his jaw.

Victory had a sweet taste. "I do believe," Charles said to Francis with a grin, "that you, Your Majesty, are in a position of checkmate."

CHARLES STOOD AT the base of the steps leading to the Convent of Santa Clara and took a deep breath.

It had been a long time since he'd visited his mother, Joanna, and as usual, he was apprehensive. He was never sure what mood she'd be in, though he would put several gold coins on it not being jovial. It never was.

"Your Majesty." A nun stood before him, her hands clasped. "The queen is ready for you."

He nodded curtly then climbed the wide, stone steps. He had in his pocket a silver necklace with a glass pendant that he'd bought in Italy. He hoped she'd like it, even if she never wore it.

"Brother! You are here."

"Catherine!" He stopped in his tracks. "I will ask a question to the contrary. What are *you* still doing here?"

"Brother, I…" His youngest sister looked down at her black gown and shifted from one foot to the other. "It's just that I…"

"It's just that you what? You deliberately disobeyed me?"

"No, not intentionally, but Mother, she couldn't do without me. She needs me here."

"But I told you…" He marched up to her, battling to control the volume of his voice. "No, make that I *ordered* you to leave for Portugal, some time ago, to marry King John. I had agreed it with him."

"I know and I am sorry I did not go."

"You are sorry. You. Are. Sorry." He removed his cap and pushed his hand through his hair. "That is not good enough. I have paid your dowry and Eleanor is long since back in Castile. I had expected this union to take place while I was otherwise engaged fighting the Italian war. I cannot do everything, sister. I need to know my instructions will be followed, by you, my family, at least. Of all people. You."

She stared up at him with wide eyes.

He fought the urge to bellow at her and kept his voice low, though it was rather growling. "I expect to be obeyed, Catherine."

"I am sorry, really, I am. And—"

"It is not her fault, Charles."

Charles turned at the sound of the Queen of Castile's voice. It was quiet and thready, but still, he'd know it anywhere. "Mother."

"Son." She held out her hands, palms down. Her long, black gown touched the floor and her black, velvet headdress was decorated with pearls.

He walked up to her and took her pale, slender hands in his. He raised the right one to his lips and kissed her. "You are well?"

"I am but a half a person. It is only by God's will that I am still strong enough to take one breath after another."

He chose to ignore her statement, for she appeared in reasonable health. "I have for you a gift. From Italy." He placed the necklace in her palm.

She studied it. "Your father gave me one like this, a long time ago."

"So you like it?"

She smiled, though it didn't reach her eyes. "I thank you for thinking of me."

"I always think of you, Mother."

"I don't know why. It is not what I deserve from you."

"Whatever do you mean?"

"I left you with your Aunt Margaret, all of those years ago. Abandoned as a young boy."

"It couldn't be helped. You and Father came to Spain to claim the throne, as was your duty." He gestured to a chair beside the fire. "Come, let us sit."

Joanna did as he'd asked and Catherine placed a woven, red blanket over their mother's lap.

"And Margaret is a devoted and loving aunt," Charles went on, keen to unburden his mother of this worry. "I wanted for nothing—neither did my sisters. Mechelan was a safe and beautiful home for us and we had the best tutors, fine food, and many hunting expeditions."

"That pleases me." Joanna nodded slowly. "Have you seen your brother of late?"

"Ferdinand? No, I am just back from a voyage. I came straight here."

"Some of the people of Castile still want him as their king," Joanna said, holding Charles's eye contact with remarkable surety. "They shout for it in the squares and beside the castle walls. I hear them. Often."

Charles sat back in his chair and wrapped his fingers tightly around the arms. "I have spent years here," he said with studied control of the tone of his voice, "learning their customs, their language, making good on my promise to make Spain the bedrock of my empire." He shook his head. "And the thanks I get is that they dare question me?"

"They dare." Joanna signaled for wine with a click of her fingers.

A servant gave her a goblet then offered Charles one.

He waved it away.

"They came to me," Joanna said with a shrug.

"Who came to you?" He sat forward.

"The rebels. They wanted me to sign away my rights as queen and pass on the crown and power to Ferdinand."

Charles bristled at the nerve of the rebels. If he found out who it had been, he'd have them hung for treason. "And what did you do?" He hardly dared ask.

Joanna was quiet as she sipped on her wine.

"Mother? Tell me."

"I ordered them to leave. I told them I would not betray my son, the emperor. Not for anything on God's Earth."

"Thank you." He paused. "But I am the rightful heir to the Kingdom of Spain. I *am* the King of Spain. That will not be taken away from me."

"But the people of Castile, some of them, see Ferdinand as theirs.

He grew up here, in Spanish court with his grandparents, the king and queen. They don't know you, Charles. They barely see you."

"Because I am overseas fighting Spain's battles, Mother. You know that."

"Yes, I do." She took another sip of her drink. "But you must be more present."

"Tell me truthfully, in your heart, that you believe it is I who should be king."

"Naturally, I believe that. You are my eldest son. Your father wished this for you and much more." She smiled sadly. "I wish he were here to see your achievements." Her eyes misted.

"Please, don't upset yourself, Mother," Catherine said, resting her hand on Joanna's lap.

"Sweet girl," Joanna said, touching Catherine's face. "You give me strength. All of my children do." She turned back to Charles. "I have discussed it with Ferdinand. I've told him to accept the crown as yours no matter what happens. I don't think he'll dispute it."

"I hope not." Charles's mind was whirring. He needed his brother on his side. He had enemies aplenty. What he needed was loyal aides, people upon whom he could depend, and who better than his siblings? "I will honor him with the Order of the Golden Fleece, to show my respect."

"That is a wise move, son."

"And send him to Flanders, to Aunt Margaret. She will be glad to know him and her council is astute."

"I agree that it would be good for him to go to Flanders, but he cannot go, not yet."

"Whatever do you mean?"

"My son, you do not have a legitimate heir. You are not married. These people cannot tolerate a king with no successor, no child even on the horizon."

"You suppose that I marry today and impregnate my bride tonight?"

Joanna's lips curved, almost into a smile. "Stranger things happen in God's rich tapestry of life."

He frowned and nodded at Catherine. "Speaking of weddings, Catherine must go to hers. King John of Portugal has waited long enough. It is my hope he has not changed his mind entirely, for I have paid the dowry."

"But I—?" Catherine's eyes widened. "But…"

"There are no *buts*, sister." Charles held up his hand. "You must perform your royal duty and marry for the good of the Habsburg bloodline."

"Marry for *your* empire, you mean." Catherine frowned.

"Your future children will benefit from the empire, do not forget that," Charles snapped.

Catherine's bottom lip protruded.

"You wish to refuse me, your emperor?"

"No, I wish to refuse you, my brother." She stood and placed her hands on her hips. "I wish to stay here with Mother."

"You can't. You will journey to Portugal tomorrow."

"No."

He stood and stared into her eyes. "Yes. I command it."

"No!"

"Yes, you will."

"I hate you," she cried. "I hate you. You send everyone away. Ferdinand, Eleanor, Isabella, and now me. You will be left sad and alone, your heart empty and barely beating. And I will not feel sorry for you. It is what you deserve."

"Catherine!" Joanna said. "Do not speak to Charles this way."

"But, Mother, it is true. I do not wish to leave you and marry a man I have never met."

"Child." Joanna set her drink to one side and stood. "I told you this day would come, and it has." She paused. "I suggest you go and make preparations to travel. Your new husband awaits."

"What? You also are sending me away!" Catherine glared at her mother and then at Charles. "This is the end of my life, you know that. I should kill myself now."

"Catherine," Charles said, reaching for her.

"No, leave me alone." She gathered her dress and stomped from the room.

When she'd gone from view Joanna shook her head. "I will miss her."

"I know, but I will visit you often, I promise. As often as I can when I am here in Spain."

"I would like that." She took his hand. "I should also like it if you visited with a wife, Charles, and the sooner, the better."

CHAPTER TWO

ISABELLA DABBED LAVENDER perfume on the delicate underside of her new sister's wrists.

"Are you sure he likes lavender?" Catherine asked.

"Yes, my brother adores it." Isabella added a touch to Catherine's neck, just below her ears. "And John will adore you on this day and forevermore."

"I hope so." She nibbled nervously on her bottom lip. "For I fear that—"

"Do not fear anything. I have a feeling you will be very happy together." Isabella stood back and studied the bride's final look. "Yes, perfect."

Catherine was simply beautiful in a long, cream gown embroidered with gold stitching. The heavy sleeves were puffed at the shoulders, the neckline low and the matching veil studded with tiny gems. She had pearls around her neck, hanging from her eyes and clasped into her hair. Her skin was almost as pale as the pearls, only a hint of rose upon her cheeks and her lips. She was a vision of perfection.

It was hard for Isabella not to feel a little jealous. She had waited so long for Charles to change his mind and propose again that she was beginning to wonder if her prayers were to be for nothing—and there had been hours of praying in their private chapel, besieging God to put her on the right path. For she could do good in the empire. She was sure of it, if only given the recognition and trust.

Hope had arrived with Catherine that at least the Portuguese monarchy was on the emperor's mind, but then Isabella realized that Catherine marrying King John and becoming Queen of Portugal actually lessoned Charles's need to marry her—now he had a robust ally in their court and children would come who had his bloodline, God willing.

"It is time," Luisa said from the doorway. Tall and slim, she had flushed cheeks from rushing around all morning.

"Thank you." Isabella nodded at her lady-in-waiting. "We are ready."

Luisa stepped into the room. She held a bunch of cream roses dripping with ivy. "Your Highness, you look like a promise wrapped up in a dream and a fantasy about to come to truth. His Majesty will find his heart lost to you the moment he sets eyes upon you."

"You always have such a way with words, Luisa," Isabella said with a smile.

"Words are all I have." Luisa handed the flowers to Catherine. "Though I thank God each day for the gift."

Catherine smelled the flowers, then Isabella took her thin veil and covered her face. "Come, it is time."

"The crowd is waiting." Luisa gestured to the door.

"'Crowd'?" Catherine gulped.

"Naturally, there is a crowd." Isabella smiled. "You are a spectacle to behold and you are to be our new queen. There is much curiosity."

Catherine nodded, hesitated, and then stepped forward.

Isabella linked her arm through Catherine's. "I wish you all the luck in the world. I really do."

"I thank you. You have been most welcoming." She hesitated. "In truth, dearest Isabella, you have made the ordeal of leaving my mother and coming to Portugal bearable."

"Only 'bearable'?" Isabella nudged her.

"No, that is not true. You have put me at ease. I am grateful that both you and the king are kind natured."

"It is how we were raised."

"A very different childhood to mine and my siblings'."

Isabella was quiet for a moment. "Tell me, is Charles kind natured?"

"Yes, of course… Well, apart from being a pompous dictator about me coming to Portugal. I had no say in it, not one word, and Mother backed him up."

"And here you are. A smiling, beautiful bride."

"Yes, here I am."

"And is Charles…?" Isabella asked.

"Please, go on?" Catherine studied Isabella.

"Is he a devout and faithful man?"

"If you mean faithful to God, yes, very. He is, after all, the King of all Christendom."

"Of course, I apologize. I meant no implication otherwise."

"You wonder if he has an eye for pretty girls, Isabella, am I right?"

They started down the long corridor that would lead them to the chapel. Flowers cascaded from urns and uniformed servants holding polished pikes stood in straight-backed silence.

"It is true he has had lovers," Catherine said in a hushed voice. "He is a man, and like all men, so I am told, he has needs."

"Mmm."

"And unlike us women," Catherine went on quietly, "taking a lover does not make him less of a marital catch."

"I will never wed another," Isabella said. "I wait only for him."

Catherine stopped and turned to Isabella, taking her hand. "You should consider other noblemen, princes, kings, for you deserve so much more from life than waiting for a man who barely knows you exist."

"I will wait."

"But he has snubbed you so, by promising his hand to the infant princess, Mary Tudor of England."

"He will not marry her. God will answer my prayers."

"How can you be so sure?"

"It is King Henry's and our aunt's feeble attempt to control Charles." She paused. "I know enough of him to know he is not a man who will be controlled."

Catherine nodded. "That is true."

"He has the King of France his prisoner, does he not?"

"Yes. That is also true. He is imprisoned in Spain."

"And Pope Clement is in the emperor's debt after his victories in Northern Italy."

"I believe I have heard that from Charles himself."

"So…" Isabella tapped her temple. "A man of that intellect and ability will soon see that I am his most attractive candidate for marriage, not least because we are close in age." She tipped her chin. "Plus, it is only I who can bring a vast dowry of cruzados to fund his wars. It is I who should give him pure-blood sons. And it is only I who has the education in politics, Christian doctrine, and etiquette to enable me to sit at his side as empress and fulfill the most regal of duties."

"I wish for nothing more, dear Isabella," Catherine said. "For you would make a fine and wise empress. Adored by peoples in lands far and wide."

"I thank you." Isabella smiled suddenly as she remembered this day wasn't about her. "But come. You keep the king waiting."

The vast ceremonial room was packed full of nobles, council, and clergy dressed in their finery. The weak winter sun filtered through the stained glass windows and incense burned, mixing with the scent of cologne and perfume.

"May God be with you every step of the way, my lady," Luisa said, fussing with Catherine's veil.

Catherine smiled. "Thank you."

"And try to enjoy this special day," Isabella said. "John will make a fine husband to you, I promise."

Catherine's smile was a little shaky, as though she were struggling to hold back tears.

"Just concentrate on his face," Isabella whispered. "When you get to the altar look into his eyes and forget about everyone else."

Catherine turned to make the long walk to her marriage—to her reign as Queen of Portugal.

She didn't move.

Her eyes were fixed on John standing with his back to her and wearing a thick, red cape, the collar lined with gray fox fur, and a scarlet cap set at an angle. He was a tall, broad man, but in this regalia, he looked like a giant.

"Would you like me to walk with you?" Isabella asked, sensing Catherine was about to run from court, never to be seen again.

"Yes." Catherine swallowed. "Yes, please."

"We women have to stick together, right?" Isabella smiled and took a step onto the red carpet that had been laid along the aisle.

A harpist began to play a gentle lullaby that reminded Isabella of birdsong.

"Come," she said under her breath, conscious now that the guests were turning to face the stationary bride. "Just one step in front of the other."

Catherine stared straight ahead and gripped the flowers, the gauzy veil thankfully hiding the fact that she'd paled further and her eyes were misted.

Then she began to walk.

With each moment that passed, Isabella's heart squeezed. She so wanted to be a bride—to be Charles's bride. It was impossible not to allow herself a moment of girlish fantasy that it was she in the beautiful, flowing gown and the bejeweled veil, holding a bouquet as she walked toward her king—her emperor.

But she shook the selfish thoughts away and rejoiced in the expression of stunned awe on her brother's face when they'd reached the altar.

It was true he'd loved Eleanor, but Catherine was also going to steal his heart. She was pretty and sweet of nature and witty too. They'd have a lot in common as time went on and Isabella was sure she'd prove herself to be a worthy queen.

The ceremony was long and drawn out, the bishop clearly enjoying having a captive audience. Hymns were sung, prayers were spoken, and vows exchanged.

By the time the feasting had begun, Isabella was grateful for the wine, cheese, and fish laid out in the Great Hall.

"Congratulations," she said to her brother as the congregation mingled. "I wish all of God's blessings upon you."

"Thank you." John kissed her cheek. "Catherine is a beautiful and pious queen for our beloved country."

"I believe you will make each other very happy." She finished the glass of wine she was holding in two big gulps. "And I will pray for healthy, strong sons to arrive at the soonest opportunity."

He raised a decanter and refilled her glass. His expression turned serious. "I wish for your happiness too. And sons. Will you not reconsider your choice of husband?"

"Not marry Charles?"

"My sweet sister, he has not talked of you for many months, not even when he sent a letter to me with Catherine. It contained only matters of politics and his empire."

She looked away, hating the fact that her throat had thickened with disappointment.

"There are other titled men in Europe who would make you a fine husband, Isabella. Give you the life you deserve."

"No." She shook her head. "I have made it clear: It is the emperor or the monastery. I will not give myself to any other than Charles Holy Roman Emperor or God. At this moment in time, I believe it will be to God to whom I pledge my eternal devotion of marriage, but there is a small part of me, a tiny seed, that is hope. Hope that Charles will see sense and come for me."

"Hope is fragile." John touched her cheek. "And when it breaks it can crumble the soul."

"Not *my* soul, for it is scaffolded in faith." She managed a stiff smile. "So do not fear for my future, for it will unfold as is God's will. Today, it is your day to celebrate and rejoice in your good fortune." She gestured to Catherine, who was speaking with Luisa. "Though please, be gentle with her when night falls. Remember she has spent many years as companion to her mother in a convent. Her knowledge of men...of married life...is even more limited than that of the usual virgin bride."

"I do not need to be reminded of such things." He slugged his wine in a sharp gesture. "And I would remind you that such matters are wholly private between a man and his wife and if you—"

"Your Majesty, a letter has arrived." A puffing courtier arrived at John's side holding forward a scroll.

In an instant, Isabella spotted the emperor's royal red seal.

"It is from the emperor," she said, her voice suddenly breathy. "And when we just spoke of him." Quickly, she crossed herself. "Dear God, you work in mysterious ways."

"It is possibly a note of congratulations," John said, snapping the seal. "Nothing more."

Isabella knew that was John's way of saying, *Don't be caught up in hope*, but she couldn't help it. The emperor had sent word to their court? Were the words she longed to hear within it? Had he finally broken his engagement with Mary?

"Please, will you read it aloud?" Isabella asked when John seemed to hold the scroll from her view.

"Yes, yes…"

"Go on, then."

He cleared his throat. "'King John, dearest cousin and most illustrious monarch of Portugal. I, Charles, Holy Roman Emperor, King of Spain, Archduke of Austria, and Lord of the Netherlands write to you this day to congratulate you on your marriage to my sister Catherine.

"'And with that marriage in mind, I propose we make this a double marriage contract in order to further our two countries' alliance.'"

"A double marriage contract?" Isabella repeated.

John continued. "'I have cancelled my engagement to Princess Mary of England and it is now my wish to marry your sister Princess Isabella of Portugal.'"

"Oh, my dear Lord." Isabella clasped her cross, kissed it, then sent her eyes heavenward. "Finally."

"There is more. Let me finish," John said. "'I would settle on a dowry of nine hundred thousand cruzados, as well as the titles of Monarch of the Canaries and Indies and Ocean Sea.'"

"That is acceptable." Isabella nodded enthusiastically and set her drink aside. She steepled her hands beneath her chin. "Isn't it?"

"Nine hundred thousand cruzados is a lot of money. And titles on top of that."

"But we have it. The money and the titles, to give to him." Isabella strained to see the scroll. "Is there more? What else does he say?"

"He says… 'We will wed in Seville within the year. As I am sure you know, I have King Francis under my control and have much to attend before I can leave Madrid. Please respond to my requests at the earliest convenience and apologize to dear Isabella for my somewhat unreliable affections of late. I intend to remedy that from this moment on.' And he signs it *Charles*."

Isabella's legs felt a little weak and her heart was thudding. Was she dreaming? Was this real? Would she wake up at any moment?

"My dear," John said, cupping her elbow. "Are you quite well?"

"Yes, yes... Oh, I think I should sit down." Was this cruel trickery? She felt sure it was. And of all the days...

Quickly, John grabbed a chair and steered her into it. He knelt at her side and clasped her hand. "Isabella, what can I get you?"

She was aware of a few guests turning their way and fanned her face with her other hand. "It is hot in here."

Catherine suddenly appeared, Luisa at her side.

"What is it?" Catherine asked with a furrowed brow.

"A letter, from your brother." John handed Catherine the scroll.

Luisa filled a goblet with wine and passed it to Isabella. "Here, drink, Your Highness."

John hovered his hand around the goblet as she took a sip.

She let the cool liquid spread over her tongue and the sweetness of the claret seemed to instill some vigor into her veins.

"My dearest Isabella," Catherine remarked loudly. "It seems your prayers have been answered." She grinned and passed the scroll to Luisa then took Isabella's hand. "My brother has finally, finally, thank the good Lord above, made a sensible decision about his life." She laughed, a little burst of emotion. "This is truly the most prestigious of days, is it not?"

Isabella smiled at Catherine's obvious joy. "Yes, yes, it really is."

CHAPTER THREE

"ARCHDUKE, YOU WILL be pleased to know the treaty is signed," Charles said, striding into the library and addressing Ferdinand. "Finally, my deepest wish for peace may be about to become a truth now that I have Francis, the aggressor, tied up with words and no longer able to wage his wars."

"He is not just captured with words," Ferdinand said, picking at a bowl of shiny, black olives and stabbing the toe of his boot into the air as he sat beside the fire. "You, brother, also have the King of France behind bars." He raised one eyebrow.

"But that is a problem." Charles poured wine. "*He* is a problem. Now that I have succeeded in humiliating him, I do not want to let him loose."

"Because you cannot trust him."

"No further than I could trust a scorpion set beneath my bed covers."

"And you have poked the scorpion by not allowing him to pay for his release."

"A cash ransom would never have worked. It had to be a deal of territory and…" Charles huffed. "And I know he'll continue to sack Italy if I release him." He glugged some wine. "Italy is now leaderless, lawless, crushed, despoiled, torn, overrun—"

"A situation you, as emperor, can rectify. Especially now that you have Pope Clement on your side."

"That is my hope." Charles walked to the window of the darkly paneled room and stared out at the Spanish skyline. The sun was setting, sending pink and lilac shards streaking over the horizon. "And having Eleanor marry King Francis is part of that plan. He has agreed to it. There was some resistance, but he knew that was futile."

"It is true, having our elder sister in French court, as queen, no less, will be a great advantage." Ferdinand nodded slowly.

"But will she be enough to ensure he abides by the treaty when I release him?"

"Perhaps that is a risk you must take." Ferdinand threw an olive into the air and caught it in his mouth.

"I am not partial to risk."

"I know that, but Eleanor is loyal to you. She will do her best."

"That is true."

"As am I." Ferdinand stood. "Loyal to you."

"And for that, I am grateful each and every day, brother." Charles paused and turned to him. "But I am sure you'll agree it is time for you to return to Flanders. I need you there taking council with Aunt Margaret. She is not getting any younger."

"I *wish* to go. My wife awaits." Ferdinand raised his eyebrows. "And I have royal duties of my own—do not forget that. Vienna is calling. Soon, we will relocate there."

"Of course." Charles turned. "And I have lingered here negotiating with King Francis and Louise of Savoy for too long."

"His mother has been an astute regent."

"As *some* mothers are."

Ferdinand nodded a little sadly. "True."

"Have you been to see our mother of late?" Charles asked.

"No." Ferdinand shook his head. "But I intend to before I leave."

"You should. She looks in fine health, physically at least, but we have no knowledge of God's plans for her."

"I will visit."

Charles squeezed his shoulder. "You are a good brother. I am glad that we know each other well in adulthood, if not in childhood."

Ferdinand stared at him, his eyes searching. "You know it still greatly unsettles the people of Castile that you have no wife...no heir. Perhaps..." He paused. "Before I leave, it is time to..."

"It is time for what, Ferdinand?"

"For you to name a successor."

"I fully intend to sire legitimate sons." Charles felt his jaw tighten. He knew that Ferdinand was pushing for himself to be that namesake.

"But until then, you need someone who can take over immediately should the worst befall you."

"It is treason to talk of the death of your emperor." There was a warning spike in Charles's voice.

Ferdinand squeezed his shoulder again as though trying to soften that spike. "Perhaps when we first met and I thought you arrogant and pompous as you stood there smugly holding your new Nuremberg musket, my words could have been considered snide, but now, now I speak only common sense, something our grandfather Maximilian was well known for. We should continue that good sense for the sake of our bloodline."

A familiar twist coiled in Charles's stomach. How could he argue? It was true. He needed heirs. He needed them soon. "I have a plan."

"You do?"

"Yes, I am marrying Isabella of Portugal. It is a good match both politically and financially." He tipped his chin. "Word has already been sent. Papal dispensation acquired. God willing, I will have a son within the year."

Ferdinand didn't hide his surprise. "I will pray for your son's speedy arrival into this world. And you will have pleased the Cortes of Castile greatly with this decision to marry within the Iberian Peninsular. It does indeed free me to leave Spain, much as I love the place of my birth." He hesitated. "But the King of England? Was he angered by the dissolution of your engagement to his daughter?"

"Of course Henry was angry." Charles waved his hand flippantly. "But what do I care? It was his own foolishness that's caused his distress. Did he really believe that I'd wait for so many years for a child to grow into a woman? No...she is not the one for me and I have heard..." He paused and closed his eyes. "I have heard..."

"What? What have you heard?"

"Eleanor told me that Princess Isabella is very beautiful, that her skin is as smooth and delicate as porcelain and her hair kissed by the colors of sunset. That her eyes brim with intelligence and that she is versed in many things." He opened his eyes and smiled. "In all honesty, I am eager to meet this bride of mine."

"And when will you wed?"

"I am journeying to Seville within days. We will have a big ceremony and much feasting. I will show her how luxuriously she will live as my empress. She will want for nothing in return for her service to the faithful people of Christendom."

"I hope you find her to be everything you dream of." Ferdinand smiled. "I really do."

A courtier appeared holding a silver tray. Upon it was a scroll.

"Where is it from?" Charles asked, reaching for it.

"An envoy from Flanders."

"Flanders?" Ferdinand looked at Charles. "I hope it is not ill news of our Aunt Margaret."

Charles tensed. His aunt had been like a mother to him, a constant and loving support. He opened the seal and quickly unfurled it. He read the few lines quickly, his mouth drying. "Here." He passed it to Ferdinand.

Ferdinand read it. "Oh, no, our poor, poor sister. Poor, sweet Bella. She was so young."

"Too young. And her children...what sadness for them."

"They are now in Margaret's care. I thank the Lord for that."

Charles was quiet as he stood with his hands on his hips, staring at a tapestry of a falcon on the hunt over the palace of Granada.

"Our sister died a true Catholic," Ferdinand said. "Margaret says so here."

"I will ask for the strength to believe that," Charles said. "Though Bella's interest in Luther's teachings are etched upon my memory." He sighed. "Perhaps I should not have ordered her so far away."

"You have a large empire—there was nowhere close by." Ferdinand paused. "But you do realize what this means."

"Yes." He sighed sadly. "We are in mourning."

"Many weeks of mourning. It would not look good to have a grand wedding while our sister's body is still warm."

"I agree." Charles reached for the scroll and threw it into the fire, watching the flames curl the edges then ash claim the writing. "But I cannot keep Isabella waiting much longer to be my bride. I have been remiss enough."

"What are you saying?"

"The wedding will be a small, private affair and we will retreat to be alone, somewhere away from prying eyes, but it will still be beautiful and befitting of an emperor and his new empress." He racked his brains. "I will think of the perfect place before the day is out."

"I am sure you will." Ferdinand stood at his side. "And I hope that you find love with Isabella, as well as gaining sons and a rich dowry."

"You have found love?" Charles peered closely at his brother.

"With Anna, yes. She is gentle and patient and the only woman I could and would ever want." He pressed his hand over his chest. "I love her very much."

Charles studied his brother's wistful expression, heard the gentle tone of his voice, and for the first time, he hoped that his heart would also be filled with love when he saw his bride, Isabella.

>>>⫷⫷⫷

CHARLES STOOD AT the entrance to the small, private chapel at the Royal Palace of Alcázar. Dusk had settled early over Seville and with it came a winter chill that cooled his cheeks. He glanced upward. The moon was a lean crescent hanging in the east.

Tomorrow, he would marry and he hoped the delicate new moon was a good omen for his fortunes. He also hoped his new bride would be as captivating as his sister had described her to be.

He stepped into the dimly lit foyer and again paused as his eyes adjusted to the candlelight.

He'd asked the clergy to make themselves scarce for his private evening worship and they'd done as instructed, leaving incense burning amongst the huge urns of frothy, white orange blossom that had been arranged ready for the marriage ceremony.

He walked along the aisle, his footfalls dull thuds on the woven carpet. When he reached the altar he bowed his head before the image of Christ and paused.

He waited.

And waited some more.

The usual sense of calm he found in church didn't come over him. Still, his heart pounded. He was full of thoughts of tomorrow, his limbs fidgeted, and his stomach was a tight knot. A thousand questions for the Holy Father about his bride sprang into his mind. These thoughts scrubbed away all of his worries about Francis, his funding of wars and armies, anxieties about his mother and siblings. All that was in his mind was Isabella of Portugal and how their first meeting would be.

The entrance door creaked.

A small gust of wind.

A footstep.

For a brief moment, irritation needled at him. He'd asked for solitude. But then he saw that it was a woman who had entered the chapel. Her small, cloaked silhouette paused, as he'd done, no doubt to let her eyes adjust to the buttery candlelight.

Barely thinking of the reason why, he ducked into a confession box to his right, the middle booth, and closed the door. He swallowed tightly and stared straight ahead.

He'd heard that Isabella and her cortege had arrived at the palace only the day before. And being a religious woman, with a strict and pious upbringing, it was no surprise she'd entered God's house the evening before her marriage.

And it was her. He knew it in his bones, in his blood, in every sinew. How, he could not explain. This was Isabella. His bride.

His breaths were shallow as her soft footfalls came closer. He hoped to hear her voice or catch the scent of her perfume—anything to know something more of her before they stood with the bishop and exchanged vows.

Would God give him that blessing?

And then one of the penitent's doors to the confession box opened. The rustle of material filled his ears and he was besieged now not just with the perfume of incense and orange blossom, but also with lavender.

His heart did a strange skip, then a beat to catch up. He clasped his hands in his lap, unused to the nerves that were running amok through his body.

"Bless me, for I am sorry for these and all my sins, Father."

He held in a gasp at the sound of her voice. Clearly, she thought him a priest awaiting her confession.

"It has been one week since my last confession," she said, her whispered voice sincere and sweet.

Charles closed his eyes and blew out a breath he hadn't known he'd been holding. "Go on," he managed.

"I have been traveling from my home in Portugal, the road long and dusty, but now I am here to marry the only man I vowed I would ever lie with at night and stand beside during the day."

"The *only* man?"

"Yes, the Holy Roman Emperor, Archduke of Austria, King of Spain." She paused. "Charles." Another pause, though the moment seemed to swell with the last word she'd uttered. His name.

"If it were not his hand being offered," she went on, "I would be entering the convent to devote my life to God. The emperor is the only mortal to whom I will ever betroth myself."

"And why is that?" Charles hardly dared hear her answer.

And she kept him waiting for several long moments before she did. "Because he is my destiny and I have saved myself entirely for him. I will be his wife, his lover, the mother of his children and on top of that, his empress."

"And are you ready for such a commitment?"

"Yes." No hesitation this time. "I am well educated and of an astute nature. I see the things that happen around me. The only thing I ask myself, and I pray for God's forgiveness, is..."

"You must say." Charles turned to his left, toward the latticed screen, and could just make out her profile through the shadows. She stared straight ahead, hands steepled as if in prayer, her fingertips touching her chin. "Tell me your sins," he whispered.

"My sin is that I wonder if he is ready for such a woman as I."

Charles nearly laughed at her words but managed to keep the sound locked inside. "A sin indeed to think...*presume*... such a thing of an emperor."

"Yes. I know, Father." She turned to face him.

Quickly, he looked away and adjusted his hood to ensure it was pulled up snugly.

"I have heard of his kind nature," Isabella said, "and ambitions for power. Of his quarrels with King Francis and his success in battles. But his empire is so vast and I fear he is not decisive enough to control his territories, especially with threats from the Ottomans."

"It is true, he is kind natured and ambitious—"

"You know him, Father?"

Charles cleared his throat. "*Of* him, my child. I know *of* him."

"Then tell me, can he summon respect for a woman who has the love and command of her people? Will he be threatened by my ability to hold council, make decisions, study facts with a curious mind?"

Charles closed his eyes and pulled in a deep breath. In that moment, he knew that he had made the right choice. Isabella, if she spoke the truth, would be someone upon whom he could depend and with whom he could leave great responsibility when he went to Rome. But one thing bothered him. "You said you fear he is not decisive enough to control his territories. Why do you think that?"

"Because it has taken him so many years to go forward with his proposal of marriage to me, his head and his heart, so it seems, flitting to other potential wives and taking many to his bed to indulge in pleasures of the flesh and—"

"That is over," Charles said, defensive and harsher than he'd intended. That was in the past and she'd have to know this. "The emperor is here, in Seville, and will marry you tomorrow. There will be no more talk of his indecision or doubts of his fidelity."

"No more talk of it?"

"No." Charles closed his eyes and blew out a breath. He took hold of the cross at his neck. "There will be no more talk of it because the emperor will, before you, before God, before many witnesses, take you, Isabella of Portugal, as his one and only love. He will honor you with body and soul and heart until the day he dies." He paused. "His loyal devotion will be greater than you can have ever imagined."

"Father...I...but how do you—?"

"The emperor knows that you will make a faithful and wise empress and will return that commitment."

"I will. Oh, I will. I will promise never to doubt him and to always be loyal and loving and..." Her words trailed off, as though she were battling to control her emotions.

Charles looked at her again, this time letting his gaze linger as he took in her small, straight nose that was perhaps a little snubbed at the end, the shape of her full lips and the thick curls of hair that lay over her shoulders. The urge to show himself, to open the door and know every detail of her face, was almost overwhelming, but he controlled his impulse.

And as much as his heart was thudding, a sense of calm washed over him. His bride was immaculate, beautiful and intelligent. He had indeed been blessed.

"Oh, mighty Lord, I am sorry for these and all my sins," she whispered, kissing a rosary. "Our savior, Jesus Christ, suffered and died for us. In His name, our Lord have mercy."

"May our Lord and God, Jesus Christ, through the grace and mercies of His love for humankind, forgive you all your transgressions." Charles clenched his fists, knowing at some point he'd have to confess his sin of pretending to be a priest, or would he? He was Holy Roman Emperor, after all. Wasn't he, surely, above everyone, allowed to take a confession?

"But, Father...what is my penance?" She turned to the delicate latticework.

Quickly, he looked away. "You have acted contrite," he managed. "And repented." He paused. "I suggest two *Hail Marys* and when you meet your new husband you look upon him without judgment for his past and only with faith in your future together."

"You are very wise, Father. I thank you and bid you goodnight." She gently set the palm of her hand against the lattice with her small fingers spread.

He covered it with his own, the need to be near to her, touch her, as acute as needing to breathe.

Suddenly, she withdrew, then stood and his heart squeezed as he dropped his hand back to his lap.

He didn't want her to leave. Sitting in the darkness, listening to her soft voice, had been magical, spiritual. A moment he'd never forget.

But it was over and she'd left the confession box, her presence seeming to take with it the warmth that had surrounded him.

He waited a moment then stood and opened the door. He was just in time to see her sweeping gracefully from the chapel, her cloak flowing and her hair streaming behind her.

Charles pressed his hand over his heart. It was fuller than it had ever been. As though the dark void that had been there was suddenly brimming with warmth, light, and hope.

His wedding day could not come soon enough. For now that he had met her, he knew he would not be complete until he held Isabella of Portugal in his arms.

CHAPTER FOUR

ISABELLA RAISED THE lavish bouquet of orange blossom to her nose and drew in the familiar, citrusy scent. The delicate, white flowers symbolized her virginity and with that, her own personal, long-held belief that Charles would eventually pick her as his bride. She was grateful he had, and also that even though the wedding ceremony had had to be quieted, she hadn't had to compromise on her choice of floral decorations.

"It is time," John said, from the door to her bedchamber. "Your new husband awaits."

"And he will not be disappointed," John's wife, Queen Catherine, said, smoothing her hand over her swelling belly. "You have never looked more beautiful, dear sister. Don't you agree, husband?"

"I do." John set his hand protectively on the small of his wife's back. "A vision to behold. I pray our parents are looking down from heaven on this day."

"I am sure they are." Catherine touched John's cheek, an intimate, loving gesture that summed up their new but deep love for one another.

"I thank you." Isabella smiled. A confident, optimistic smile. The king and queen were proof that political matches could also be love matches. Also, since her confession the night before in the palace's private chapel, she'd experienced a new sense of calm. Her nerves had been soothed by the soft voice of the priest. He'd made her feel safe, heard, and justified to have waited patiently for Charles to come to her.

Which meant she'd slept well, risen early, and broken her fast with bread, eggs, and olives. And as the sun crept higher, she knew she was on her final moments of maidenhood.

"Here." Luisa fussed with Isabella's black, lace mantilla veil, straightening invisible creases. "It is time to cover your face."

"And pray to God the emperor likes what he sees when it is removed." Isabella stood still as the veil was drawn, giving her a gauzy view of the world. The veil matched her silk dress to perfection, the lace details continuing on the cuffs of the black sleeves and around the neckline.

"How could he not like what he sees? He is a lucky man." John held out his elbow. "Allow me to walk you to your imperial husband."

Hushed conversation murmured toward Isabella as she arrived at the entrance to the chapel. Her stomach fluttered with anticipation and she had to concentrate on steady, deep breaths.

"I am sorry it is not the fanfare we'd hoped for, you becoming an empress," John said. "Mourning has dulled the festival of the occasion, but hopefully, that will not shadow your joy."

"It will not, for it does not matter. The outcome is the same, whether or not there are crowds, trumpets, and straining tables of food. I will still be Charles's empress at the end of today."

"And for many days to come." John squeezed her hand. "Are you ready?"

"Yes." She swallowed tightly and clutched her bundle of flowers. "I am."

A harpist began to play.

Her brother walked her through the entrance she'd stepped into in near darkness the night before. Now it was light and when she looked at the small congregation, their faces were lit by the sun streaming through the rose window. But her attention didn't linger on the wedding guests, or the bishop, or the lavish floral decorations, it went straight to the man standing at the end of the aisle with his back to her.

He was tall and broad and his red, velvet cape held his great coat of arms—an elaborate crest showing a shield of flags signifying all of his lands, behind which soared a black eagle with two heads, the wings fanning out in great, feathery flicks. His boots were also black, as was the beret set upon his dark hair.

She concentrated on putting one foot in front of the other, glad of the veil that gave her a sense of concealment from the curious eyes turning her way.

A step before she reached her groom, he turned to face her.

Her breath hitched and her stomach tightened. Her heart beat so fast, she wondered if it would fly right out of her chest.

Charles was indeed a handsome man. His features were strong and angular and his skin clear. His lips were tipped in a slight smile and his kind eyes studied her curiously.

Around his neck, he wore the heavy insignia of the Order of the Golden Fleece, and his cape was held in place with a heavy, golden buckle. He reached out his hand, signet rings on two of his fingers, and allowed John to place her small hand in his.

This first touch had her knees weakening, the moment suddenly so real…finally. After all of the years of waiting and hoping.

"Before God, and as king, I give you the hand of my sister Princess Isabella of Portugal," John said. "And I trust, that before God, you will promise to always treat her with respect and kindness."

"I will," Charles said, his attention still firmly on Isabella. "That is my promise before God and to you, King John of Portugal."

John stepped away.

Isabella took a deep breath and locked her knees, hoping she didn't look as though she were swaying. She gripped the stems of her flowers.

Charles tipped his head slightly, as though trying to see through the haze of the veil.

She sucked in a breath, composing herself. This was the face she would look at until her dying day. She knew that in her heart.

"Kings, queens, lords, ladies, noblemen, and councilors," the bishop said in a booming voice. "We are gathered here today in the house of the Lord Almighty to witness the marriage of Charles of the House of Habsburg, our most illustrious Holy Roman Emperor, to Princess Isabella of Portugal. Now, if you would all join me in a prayer of commitment and thanks…"

There was a shuffle to Isabella's right as people knelt or bowed their heads.

Charles continued to stare straight at her.

She blinked, emotion welling, and was glad of the long prayer the bishop read out as a chance to recover herself from the overwhelming moment.

When he'd finished a hymn was sung by a choir, the words all melting into one for Isabella.

"And now for the vows," the bishop said, turning the page of his small, red book. "Now if you could—"

"I know what to say," Charles said, his voice sure and steady. "Thank you, Bishop."

"Oh…well…of course." The bishop cleared his throat and closed his book.

"I, Charles, take you, Isabella, to be my empress, my wife, to be the mother of our children, to be the companion of my heart from this breath until my last. I promise to love you and to be true to you in good times and in bad and to cherish our time together on God's sweet Earth." He moved closer and took a hold of her veil. Then slowly, very slowly, he lifted it, revealing her face.

For a moment, she felt shy, naked, but then he smiled and a new softness filled his eyes.

"My beautiful bride," he said quietly, almost as if the congregation weren't there at all. "I promise to forsake all others, to know only you in my bed from this day forward."

She nodded slightly. How had he known that was such a worry for her?

"Do you believe me?" he asked.

"Yes."

"Good, because it is a truth." He pressed one hand to his chest, his fingers pressing the heavy, golden chain of his insignia against his cloak.

"Princess," the bishop said.

She nodded, and with a sure and steady voice, said, "I, Princess Isabella of Portugal, take you, Charles, Holy Roman Emperor, to be my husband, to be the father of our children, to be the companion of my heart from this breath until my last. I promise to love you and to be true to you in good times and in bad and to cherish our time together on God's sweet Earth."

Charles smiled, his lips curling easily, as though it was something he did often, and small creases darted from his eyes to his temples. He still had a boyish look despite his twenty-eight years.

"The rings." The bishop held his leatherbound book forward, two rings set upon it. He made the sign of the cross over them.

Isabella reached for the larger, golden one and placed it on Charles's right ring finger. "With this ring, I further pledge commitment to our unity."

He looked at it for a moment, fingers spread, as though unused to a jewel on that finger, then he reached for the other blessed ring.

He took her right hand in his and held the ring at the tip of her finger. "With this ring, I further pledge commitment to our unity."

Her stomach tightened as he slipped it on, hardly able to believe that she was finally his empress, his wife. And she could tell that his heart was kind. Despite his great power and vast lands, he was a good man with a moral compass steered by his faith.

"I now pronounce you husband and wife," the bishop said, his voice suddenly loud. "And I give you, dear flock"—he cast his arms wide—"the illustrious emperor and his celebrated empress."

There was sudden loud clapping and a few shouts of congratulations.

Isabella smiled, tension slipping from her shoulders and her heart swelling with joy.

Charles, seeming to utterly ignore the commotion, moved closer still and cupped her face in his big, warm hands. "We should get one thing straight between us," he said, his face so close, she could feel his breath. His gaze bored into hers with an intensity that heated her from the inside out.

"We should?" She felt consumed by him in that moment. He was all she saw.

"Yes…" he whispered against her lips. "I am already hopelessly, fervently, ridiculously in love with you."

And then he kissed her. A soft press of his warm lips as he held her face tenderly.

She dropped her flowers to the altar floor and clutched his shoulders, feeling, beneath the thick material of his cape, his solidity and strength.

He loved her.

Already.

It was more than she could have ever dared hope. For she knew in her heart, she loved him. She had always loved him. She'd been created to be his wife. She knew that in her soul. And now here they were, married, a lifetime of love and, God willing, children ahead of them.

He pulled back, his eyes flashing, pupils wide, and swept his tongue over his bottom lip, as though searching for any lingering taste of her. "We should receive our congratulations."

She nodded. Though what she really wanted was for him to kiss her again.

"And we should feast," he said, "though you should know that I will spend these daylight hours consumed by the anticipation of our first night together."

"You will?" The nerves she'd pushed away each time she'd thought of lying with Charles suddenly reared their head.

"Yes." Stooping, he reached for her bouquet. He brought it to his nose and breathed deep. "But do not fear, Isabella, for I will ensure your first time is as pleasurable for you as it is for me."

A strange tingle went down her spine, filling her with a new sense of need that weighed heavily in her abdomen. It wasn't unpleasant—in fact, she wanted to explore it more.

Dressed as Charles was in his finery, she couldn't imagine him naked, yet later, when the sun set she wouldn't have to imagine. She'd get to find out if the whispered morsels of bedchamber information about men were true.

"Here." Charles handed her the flowers. "Give me your hand, my love."

She took the bouquet and felt his hand wrap around hers.

He turned to their audience, who were still clapping and calling. He waved and stepped down from the altar.

Isabella went with him, smiling at her brother and his wife, at Luisa, and then some of the noblemen who had traveled from Lisbon for the ceremony.

She felt as though she were floating as she walked from the chapel, happiness filling every corner of her body and soul. As they entered the Gothic-style courtyard, a few courtiers threw rice at their feet, sending them good wishes for fertility.

"Thank you, thank you," Charles called jovially.

Three trumpeters on a balcony started to play. Flags holding the image of Charles's family crest hung from their instruments.

Charles waved up at them then turned to Isabella with a smile. "It is beautiful here in Seville, and had I not been in mourning, we would have spent the first moon of our marriage feasting and hosting and taking to the streets in carriages so the people could see their new empress, but I fear that is not going to be possible."

"I understand, and I am sorry for your loss."

He dipped his head, his eyelids heavy for a moment. "The loss of my sister is a sadness my whole family will have to bear."

"God rest her soul."

He pulled in a deep breath. "So I have decided, we will go to Granada."

"Granada?"

"Yes, to the Palace of Alhambra. It is the only place I can think of that will be beautiful enough for my beautiful bride."

"I thank you for the compliment."

"It is not a compliment—it is a truth." He ran the back of his index finger around her jawline, slowly, delicately.

Her breath caught and her nipples tingled. She was his to touch, and already, he appeared to like touching her.

"I have spent many nights wondering about you, Isabella," he said quietly, "imagining you in my dreams, but now…now I know I would never have been able to dream up such beauty, such regal-ness, for you are truly exquisite, and I have to confess…" He frowned.

"Go on."

"I have to confess that I know now how remiss I was in not marrying you sooner. I hope you will forgive me for my delays and dallying and that you will let me make it up to you."

"There is nothing to make up for. We stand here, on this day, as man and wife, do we not?"

"Yes." He stepped closer and rested his hands on her waist. "But my empress deserves the best of everything I can give. And when we reach the palace in Granada I will ensure we are free to be together, solely and undisturbed." His smile dropped for a split second but then was back. "And I will pray to God that you will find a piece of your heart with which to love me, even just a little."

CHAPTER FIVE

"**H**AVE YOU FINISHED with the lavender water, Your Majesty?" Luisa asked from the shadows of the bedchamber.

"Yes. Thank you." Isabella lifted her right foot from the warmth and set about drying it. She'd washed from head to toe, glad of the freshness the water gave her body after the long, hot day.

Luisa took the water to the door and handed it to a servant. She then closed the door and picked up Isabella's brush. "Shall I?"

"Yes, please." Isabella placed the towel to one side and sat up straight. Luisa had brushed her hair many times and the ritual of the act was always comforting.

But as Luisa started on this night, Isabella found the knots in her shoulders and the nerves in her belly not relaxing in the slightest. She clasped her hand in her lap, the material of her white, silk undergarment bunching around her fists.

"Are you anxious about what will come tonight?" Luisa asked quietly.

"Would you be?"

"The emperor is a virile man of standing and strength whose need to sire sons is well noted," Luisa said. "Which would make me anxious, yes."

Isabella was silent. If she'd hoped Luisa would offer words of comfort, she'd had none.

"However," Luisa went on, "I have watched the way his eyes

move with you on this first day of your marriage. How he seems to have not needed or had time for anyone else at his wedding, other than you. I'm not saying he's been impolite, but for me at least, it's clear he would have been happy for everyone to have left so he could have you, his new empress, to himself."

"Which he will have...soon." She glanced at the darkened window. The thin moon was peeking over a church steeple.

"And you must take a deep breath and relax yourself for him, if you don't mind me giving you that advice."

"I'll take all the advice I can get." Isabella huffed slightly. "For I have only snippets of knowledge of what is to come. Tiny morsels of information given to me almost reluctantly by my mother."

"Your husband is the best person to fill you in on the details, not me, not your dearly departed mother." Luisa kept on brushing Isabella's long hair. "Don't you agree?"

"Yes, of course." *Take a deep breath and relax*, was that really the best advice she had? Maybe it would be best to close her eyes and think of something else—if she could through the pain she feared the act would entail—and wait for his seed to plant itself.

"I do know..." Luisa said, pausing what she was doing, "that it can be quite pleasurable for both parties."

"From whom have you heard this?"

"I have a married friend who laments her husband's long tours away with the army. She wishes to have him in her bed every night, as her husband...as her lover."

"So she enjoys it?"

"Yes, and I believe you will too. Your husband is an emperor, after all, quite excellent at everything he does. Why should bedding his wife be any different?"

Knock. Knock.

The door that connected her bedchamber to Charles's opened. He stood there wearing only brown breeches held up by a thick, leather belt. His wide, tanned chest was naked, as were his feet. He ran a hand through his hair, damp by the looks of it, and looked straight at Isabella.

"I will leave you, alone, Your Majesty." Luisa set down the brush. "I bid you goodnight."

"Goodnight," Isabella managed. Suddenly, she felt like prey, as though her lady-in-waiting were leaving her to the wolves of the night. She tried and failed to suppress a shiver, even though she wasn't cold. The room was warm; a fire blazed in the grate.

Luisa left the room, the door shutting with a definite *clunk* behind her.

Charles stepped farther in the room. He glanced at the window, as though checking they had privacy, as the curtains hadn't been drawn.

They were in the highest rooms overlooking nothing but the tiled, orange roofs of the city beyond.

"The new moon is a good sign," Charles said.

"It is a sign the earth will soften within the next weeks," she said. "For sowing to begin."

He didn't reply. Instead, he walked over to her and took her hands. Gently, he pulled her to standing.

"I like your hair like this." He took a strand between his thumb and finger and spread it out. "Loose and framing your face."

She didn't reply. The truth was wearing just a thin undergarment, she felt almost naked before him.

Which of course was what he wanted.

"Do not fear what is to happen," he said, his finger sliding over her collarbone to the cross that sat in the dip of her throat. "It is perfectly natural."

"I do not fear it."

"So why are you pale? Your cheeks were flushed earlier, when we feasted."

"It must have been the wine."

"Because you didn't like it?" He raised his eyebrows. "I had it ordered especially. The finest quality. For you."

"It was delicious."

"Would you like some now?"

"No, no, thank you." She swallowed tightly. "And it might be natural for you, but I—"

"You are a virgin, as your brother promised me. But, my love, I am a man, halfway through my life. You must know that I am not."

She nodded.

"But do not look at that as a disadvantage." He smiled and bit on his bottom lip.

"Why shouldn't I?"

"Because at least one of us knows what we're doing."

She didn't answer because he drew his finger downward, over the dip of her throat, until he reached the lace that held together the top of her undergarment. "Charles," she managed. "But...I..."

"You are supposed to want me as much as I want you," he said softly as he pulled the lace gently. "That is how this will work best."

"I *do* want you."

Again, he smiled. "Saying it doesn't make it real." He pulled the lace some more and the material gaped, showing the first rise of her breasts.

Her nipples poked forward, hard, little points that ached.

"But I will make that want in you real." He moved closer so his lips hovered over hers. "You will want me. You will be begging for me. That is my promise."

Before she could answer, he kissed her. It wasn't as chaste as his kiss in the chapel. Now, there was a touch of his tongue and he slanted his head to make it deeper.

She curled her hands into fists at her sides, wishing she could relax.

He pulled back, smiling as he looked into her eyes, then looked down at her breasts. The silk had fallen open and her pert breasts were exposed.

"How sweet you are," he whispered, then he stroked the back of his thumb over her left nipple.

She gasped at the strong, heavy sensation that traveled through her breast.

"I want to touch you all over," he said, stroking the side of her breast now, then tracing the delicate flesh underneath and to her sternum. "I want to know every inch of you better than I know myself."

Isabella locked her knees and fluttered her eyes closed. His caress was so soft and gentle. "I want that too."

"Do you? Do you really?"

She opened her eyes. "Yes. It is what I have dreamed of and prayed for."

"*Prayed* for?" He raised his eyebrows. "What an indecent prayer."

"What? I... Oh... Well, I mean..."

He chuckled. "Do not worry yourself. I am sure God hears prayers of all manner of things."

Gently, he pinched her right nipple, urging it harder still.

Oh, and she liked the sensation. She hadn't expected to, but it seemed to grow, pulling with it heat that went through her body, settling between her thighs.

"Your body responds to me," he said, "as mine is responding to you."

He released her nipple and pulled the last of the lace free. Her clothing slipped downward, falling from her arms to settle on her hips.

He blew out a breath and stepped to the side, studying her as he moved slowly around her.

She stared straight ahead, at the stars now showing themselves beside the moon.

"Your beauty has rendered me speechless," he said, coming up close behind her. "I can barely believe the good fortune with which I have been graced."

"I am pleased to please you."

The heat of his chest blazed against her bare back. She was sure he'd be able to hear the thudding of her heart.

"Oh, you please me immensely, Isabella. I could not want or ask for more." He slid his hands to her hips then pushed at her undergarment.

It fell from her hips, pooling around her feet.

She tensed and squeezed her legs together.

"You should not be shy about showing me your body," he said, curling his arms around her waist and embracing her fully. "For all I see is magnificence."

He kissed the curve of her neck, whispering touches of his lips that sent need flowing over her flesh.

She sighed and closed her eyes. A log shifted in the grate.

"Can you feel me?" he asked, pulling her against him. "How much I want you?"

A hard wedge of flesh pressed against her lower back.

"Yes," she said, her voice breathy. "But...oh...I don't know, I..."

"Shh," he said into the shell of her ear. "You don't need to know. I will show you."

His kisses spread to her neck again, then lower, to her shoulder, down her back. Peppering little touches of his lips. He stooped so he was kissing a trail down her spine, the curve of her lower back, and then over her buttocks.

"Oh...Charles," she said, reaching for the post of the bed for support. "What...? I...?"

He didn't reply. Instead, he swept his hands from her ankles up her legs, to the curve of her hips. Then he applied pressure, turning her to face him.

She stared down at his face so shockingly close to her private parts.

"You taste like flowers," he murmured, then he tipped forward and kissed her pubic hair.

"Charles!" She gasped again, clutching his head. "What are you doing?"

He looked up at her, a sinful grin playing with his mouth. "I am learning the shape of my wife in the best way I know how." He kissed her again, just below her navel this time, then began to rise, kissing her abdomen, her sternum, her throat, and finally her mouth.

His tongue found hers and slicked against it.

She gripped his hard shoulders and closed her eyes, enjoying his kiss.

A low groan rumbled from his chest and his unmistakable sound of longing thrilled her. A sudden rush of confidence besieged her and she squeezed in closer to him, dancing her tongue with his.

"We have waited too long for this," he said, his eyes sparkling with passion. "It is time."

He pulled her to the bed, tipping her onto it then spreading himself over her. She was damp between her thighs and her skin felt more alive than ever, as though magic dust had been cast over it.

"I want to give you sons," she said, touching her palms to his cheeks. "It is my dream for us."

"I want that too." He moved a strand of hair from her brow. "But there is no reason we can't have fun making them."

"So show me...show me this...fun."

He grinned. "I intend to, Empress." He slipped his hand between their bodies, loosening and then shoving at his breeches.

Once naked, he settled over her again. "Open your legs. Wider."

She did as instructed.

"Wider still."

She didn't move.

"Please do not be shy, my love."

She hitched in a breath. "Like this?" She drew up her knees, opening herself for him.

"Yes." He kept most of his weight held off her. "And let me in. Don't tighten against it."

"I'll try not to." She stared up at him and gripped his defined biceps. "I want this. I really do."

The tip of his cock nudged her wet entrance. "I believe you." He stilled and closed his eyes, groaning. "Oh, yes, I believe you."

She didn't know what had changed for him to believe her now, but when he curled his hips and entered her that first inch she gasped and held her breath.

"No," he said, "don't hold your breath. We're going slow, much as it's killing me."

"Why is it killing you?" She pressed her hand over his upper chest. "I don't want that."

"It is just the desire I feel for you. I want to get inside you, so deep, stay there until you are crying out my name in pleasure."

"I...I want that too." She curled her arms around his torso and drew her knees higher.

He slipped in some more and she willed her muscles to relax. Instead, they fluttered around his cock, seeming to adjust to having him there. "I am too tight." She gasped.

"No...No, you are perfect." He kissed her and went a little deeper.

She was getting used to his invasion now. It was not the pain she'd feared; it was dense and hot and satisfying and she wanted more.

"Do you need me to stop?" he asked. "Go slower?"

"No. No." She slid her hands down the plains of his back, into the dip and then to his buttocks. For a moment, it crossed her mind that she shouldn't touch him there, but then she remembered he'd kissed her behind and besides...he was hers as much as she was his.

So she gripped his taut buttocks and canted her hips, taking him deeper still.

"Oh, Lord, give me strength." He groaned, giving her more. "I am going to want you every night for the rest of our lives, like this, just like this..."

"It feels so good," she whispered against his lips. "Don't stop."

"I won't."

He set up a gliding rhythm, rubbing her inside and out. A pressure began to grow in her cunny. It was pleasant, but also urgent and greedy.

"Oh," she gasped. "I had no idea...that it would feel...like this."

"We are perfect together," he murmured, his body hard as stone, tense, as though he were holding himself under tight control. "And I want you to find pleasure, especially this first time."

He was staring down at her intently.

"I am—it is. Pleasurable, that is."

"There's more. Take it, ride the crest of sensation that grows until it's overwhelming, and then let it crash around you."

"Crash around me?" She let out a groan. "Oh...oh, yes, there...just there..."

"Yes, that's it, let it grow." He ground up against her harder, rubbing the swollen nub that had become so demanding and needy.

She closed her eyes and gritted her teeth, dragging her fingers up his back to clutch his shoulders again.

"I am yours," he said hotly. "In this moment, nothing else exists except for you and I."

"And I am yours." She hooked her legs behind his and his cock drove to new depths. She was so wet and pliant for him, but she didn't care if that was wrong because the pressure was sublime and the crest he'd spoken of was growing, rising, almost at its peak.

"That's it," he encouraged. "Let it take you. Think of nothing else but sensation."

"Oh...oh..." The force within her was so great, she was panting, writhing, clinging to him. "I am... It's..."

She cried out. Bliss flooded her body and her cunny spasmed around his cock. She shook and trembled and bright lights flashed before her eyes.

"Argh…yes…yes…" He shouted into the crook of her neck, his cock seeming to pulse inside of her. "In the name of…"

On and on she rode her ecstasy, in awe that her body had the capacity for such pleasure. Her breaths were hard to catch, her heart beat like a bird battling to get out of a cage, and she clung to Charles's perspiring body as though he were a raft in a storm at sea.

"Isabella," he said, lifting up to look down at her face. He was breathing hard, as though he'd just been fighting in battle.

"Charles." She stroked his hair back from his brow. Shadows from the fire danced in his eyes and over his features. "Did I do it…right?"

"Perfect." He smiled through his rapid breaths. "You are so giving, so sweet, so tight… You tested my stamina in a way it never has been."

"What does that mean?" She frowned. "Is that a good or bad thing?"

"It means it was so good, I almost lost my mind to you as well as my heart and body."

"Oh…I am sorry. I think."

He laughed. "Do not be sorry, for I would not change this night, this moment, for all the gold coins in the world."

CHAPTER SIX

THE NEXT MORNING, they set off for Granada and the Palace of Alhambra. When Isabella had woken and looked out at the beautiful ornate courtyard and elegant chapel in which they'd married, she couldn't understand why Charles was so insistent they move on. Surely, they would be comfortable here in Seville for any length of time.

But insistent Charles was and after he was sure everything had been packed and organized—it seemed he liked to manage things in fine detail—they mounted two bay steeds and set off at the head of their cortege.

Mules pulled wagons full of trunks of clothes, food, and apothecary. Two dozen knights rode white horses, animals and men in full armor, helmets and manes decorated with gold and red plumes. A cart pulled crates of chickens and two pigs were also on for the ride. Mixed into the group were courtiers and servants also on horseback.

It would take three days to make the journey east to Granada. Isabella would be glad when they arrived.

"I am thankful Queen Catherine agreed for Luisa to travel with me," Isabella said to Charles as they navigated a wide track through a shaded forest. "She is also very fond of her."

He wore black breeches and an armored vest over a scarlet tunic. Attached to his leather belt was a long, sheathed sword that rested on his thigh. He adjusted his black cap and turned to her. "I am grateful too. I sense she is your friend as well as a lady-in-waiting."

"Yes, I have known her for many years. I find her quite fascinating."

"You do?" He appeared surprised.

"Yes, she has a brilliant mind for poetry." Isabella smiled. "Something that interests me."

"It does?"

"Yes."

He chuckled. "I have so much to learn about you, and I suspect learn *from* you."

"You had a fine education, with your aunt."

"Indeed. She employed only the best scholars." Charles nodded.

"And your father, did you learn much from him?"

"If you recall, I was only six when he died." Charles turned to look straight ahead. "So I can't say that I did. Nothing that was of use, anyway."

The set of his mouth told her not to pry, so she took a different approach. "How about your grandfather, the great Maximilian?"

Charles seemed to relax slightly. "Yes, from him, I did learn, although he was a busy man with many lands thanks to his sometimes risky policy of maximum expansion."

"Why do you think it risky?" She was genuinely curious.

"He was constantly on the hunt for more power. Intent on taking as much land and as many titles as he could, but when he had it, he had to wait for heirs to come along to rule it."

"He did well with male grandsons. Both you and Ferdinand have control of the Spanish and the Austrian Habsburg line now."

"Yes, though Ferdinand has not been overly happy since his recent move to Austria. Now he is insisting on transporting his beloved Spanish horses to Vienna. Apparently, the Italian breeds are not to his liking."

"Why not bring his horses, if it is what he wants and he has the means to?"

"It seems it is what he desires more than almost anything—though of course a son with his wife, Anna, is his true priority."

"I will pray that happens for him."

"Look." Charles pointed forward. "A goshawk. Can you see it?"

Isabella peered forward and saw a ghostly bird with an enormous wingspan moving silently through the trees. Its belly was pale and dotted and its eyes flashed her way. "Yes, yes, I see it."

"They are exceptionally good hunting birds. I hope to fly one in Granada."

"You intend to hunt while we are there?"

"Yes, some of the time." He paused and smiled at her, leaning a little closer. "Though like my brother, I intend to work on creating sons."

She felt her cheeks flush as memories of the night before came rushing back. From all the fragments of information she'd accumulated about wedding nights, what she'd imagined could not have come close to what was. Charles had made her feel things she hadn't known she was capable of feeling. Taken her to places she hadn't known existed. And now she was looking forward to being alone and naked with him again to see what other things he had in store for her inexperienced body.

He was studying her as though amused by her blush. "I hope that plan will please you."

She cleared her throat and tightened her grip on the reins. "I intend to be a good and dutiful wife."

He laughed softly. "I believe that will come naturally."

"As will being empress. It is my destiny. It is what my mother planned for me."

"So, Empress, can you help me with a dilemma?"

They had come to the end of the woodland and before them, the track wound down through a valley of vineyards. "Of course. If I can."

"You know I hold the King of France a prisoner in Madrid?"

"Yes, I had heard," she said.

"He is an angry man, power-hungry too, which makes him dangerous." Charles paused and rubbed his chin. "We have signed a treaty, together, with which I have come off very favorably. Peace should be maintained, but…"

"But you do not trust him to keep his side of the deal."

"No." He frowned her way. "I do not. He would put a knife in my back as quickly as I saved him from a bloodthirsty mob of soldiers."

"That hardly seems Christian."

"It is what I must deal with." He clicked his tongue on the roof of his mouth. "Though I cannot keep him behind locks and bars forever…or perhaps I can."

"You cannot. It is asking for another war with France and much blood will be spilled." She thought for a moment. "So take something of his that is dear to him and hold it in his place."

"What do you mean?"

"He has sons, does he not?" An idea was forming in her mind.

"Yes, two. They are young, but not infants."

"And to a king, sons are his most precious possessions, so do a trade. Release Francis and in his place lock up his sons."

"Hold them hostage?"

"Yes. And if he breaks the treaty…" She didn't want to finish that sentence. "Which hopefully he won't because he'd know it would not be in his sons' favor."

"Mmm." Charles nodded slowly. "That is a good idea and it would get me out of the position of holding a king prisoner yet not make me too vulnerable to his madness and vengeance."

Isabella was quiet, sensing the cogs of his mind were turning.

"Francis and Henry, those are his sons' names." Charles nodded. "But I fear I will make enemies for myself in the future should I take them prisoner."

"That might be the case, but treat them well, educate them, and you might even earn some loyalty from them."

"I cannot imagine that, but yes, I believe I will discuss this idea with my council." He reached his hand between their horses.

She placed hers in it.

"I thank you, Empress, for your insightfulness and wisdom. That is not a solution I would have thought of and I have been pondering the situation for many days."

"I am glad to be of use. And I do hope to be of more use than just being a baby vineyard." She nodded at the vines and retook her reins.

He laughed. "Baby vineyard? My beautiful wife, you are already everything to me. More than I could have ever hoped or imagined. It is I who wishes to be more for you." He paused. "I intend to make up for every day I kept you waiting. What a fool I was."

"It is life's rich tapestry." She shrugged.

"I like that you see it that way, but it will not stop me from showing you my undying devotion from this day to my last to make up for my failings." He shook his head as he studied her. "What a fool I was."

⫸⫷

FINALLY, AFTER A bone-weary journey with cold nights in tents and hot days on horseback, they arrived at the vast fortress that was the Palace of Alhambra.

Over the turrets and ramparts, steeples, and slanting, tiled roofs, the sun had streaked the sky orange, and in the distance mountains loomed, their peaks coated with snow.

"It is so big," Isabella said as they rode up a cobbled lane toward it. "Enormous. A large town is within it, surely."

"Yes, the Moors certainly didn't lack imagination when it came to buildings, nor creativity. It has its own water supply, which is very reliable, as well as public baths and workshops of every kind. It is an

63

independent city with a total of six smaller palaces within it." Charles looked up at the imposing walls and even higher watchtowers that led them into the complex. "Ferdinand and Isabella made it their Royal Court after Reconquista, reclaiming it for Spain."

"They claimed many things for Spain."

"For Spain and for us." He smiled. "Look how our flags fly."

Overhead, a sea of flags fluttering lazily in the evening breeze lined the walk up to the huge, stone entrance that led into the palace grounds. Above the horseshoe arch was a carving showing a hand with five extended fingers. An image she didn't recognize but was clearly important to the Moors.

Rows of armed soldiers holding pikes upward and staring straight ahead held serious expressions as the arriving horses' hooves clattered past them, and the wagons' wheels rattled.

"Finally, we will have a bedchamber with privacy, and a marital bed," Charles said as they navigated up a steep ramp. "I am sorry for your long and tiring journey so soon into our marriage."

"It could not be helped." She smiled, trying not to show how exhausted she was, how her spine ached, her limbs dragged heavily, and her eyelids could barely be kept open. Three days in the saddle over hills and through valleys had been long enough.

She tried and failed to suppress a yawn as they entered a rectangular plaza, its four walls an arcade of arches, the lower half of which were decorated with blue and white tiles. They came to a stop beside a fountain.

"We are here. Soon you can rest," Charles said, frowning at her. "My love, you are quite pale."

"I apologize. I really don't feel..." She could barely find the words. Suddenly, she felt so weak. As though she'd managed to ride the last few hours on willpower alone, but now that she didn't need to stay atop her horse, her body had given up.

"Isabella!" Charles jumped off his horse, his feet landing with a *thump* on the sandy-stone ground.

Her peripheral vision had black specks dancing in it and her head was floating. She tried to stay upright but found herself slumping forward.

And then Charles's strong arms were around her, pulling her from the horse. He was shouting instructions to servants and courtiers, but his voice sounded as though it were far away.

She gave up and closed her eyes, succumbing to the overwhelming need to black out. Her faith in him to catch her, hold her, was absolute.

"My love," he whispered against her head. "I've got you. You're safe."

She mumbled something—she wasn't sure what. Gratitude filled her heart. Relief that her husband was a good and caring man. Strong too, for now she was scooped into his arms, against his chest. When they'd gotten closer to Granada and the threat of bandits had diminished he'd removed his armor. Now she was pressed against the soft material covering his warm body. His muscles were solid around her, unyielding, holding her as though she weighed almost nothing. He still held the lingering scent of the sage soap he used, though now it was mixed with sunshine and leather.

"You will soon be resting in the cool," he said, striding forward. "The journey is over now, I promise."

She curled her fists into his tunic and let her head rest heavily in the crook of his neck.

"Luisa, follow me," Charles called over his shoulder. "Alvaro, bring our trunks through the wine gate, to the palace's royal quarters."

"Yes, Your Majesty," Alvaro responded with his usual clipped manner. He was a trusted servant of Charles's and he was never far away.

But Isabella couldn't concentrate on the business of the servants; it took all her time to breathe in and out, though thankfully, the black dots had gone from her vision.

"I blame myself entirely," Charles said. "I asked too much of you after the journey from Lisbon to Seville, from which you had barely recovered."

"It is not your fault," she murmured. "Please don't say it is."

"I will make it up to you, I promise." He huffed. "Something I seem to have to do a lot of when it comes to you, but do not fear, I am good for my word."

"I know you are." Whizzing past her was the interior of the palace. Walls the color of burnt orange peel that had intricate stucco designs on every curve and pillar. Strange calligraphy adorned small, stone canvases, and the sound of trickling water was all around.

"We will be comfortable here," Charles said, entering the shade of a building. "And when you are stronger you will enjoy the view."

"I think I can walk."

"You might think that, but I will not risk my precious empress falling." He continued to stride. "I am keeping you in my arms, where I know you are safe."

Isabella didn't argue; the tone of Charles's voice told her it would be futile.

The sounds of the courtyard faded as they entered a large bed-chamber. The scent of sandalwood filled the air and candles flickered in darkened corners.

"I wish you to rest," Charles said, gently setting her on a wide, soft bed. "I will see you in the morning."

"No. Wait." She grasped his wrist. "Please. We have spent these last nights apart as we traveled. I wish to lie with you."

"You are not strong enough." He frowned, the shadows dancing on his face.

"I assure you I will be." She swallowed, her mouth dry. "After I have eaten something and Luisa has helped me refresh."

He shook his head. "I could not forgive myself if I delayed your recovery."

"You won't... Don't you see? I will feel worse if you leave me. I need you. I need my husband."

He cupped her face and stared into her eyes. "And I need you too." Very gently, he set a kiss on her lips. "I have some things to attend to, then I will return."

CHAPTER SEVEN

C HARLES STARED UP at the intricate dome in the ceiling above the royal bed. Created out of hundreds of tiles, it reminded him of the Spanish sky on a moonless night. It seemed to sparkle and the more he looked, the more tiny, bright points he could see.

Isabella stirred beside him and he shifted his attention to her sleeping face. She was so beautiful in sleep, her eyelashes were long and feminine, her skin as delicate as the first fall of snow, and her lips, slightly parted, temptingly kissable.

She'd been asleep when he'd climbed into bed and with her reddish hair freshly brushed and fanned out on the pillow, she'd looked like an angel. He'd once again sent a prayer to heaven to thank the Lord that he'd been so lucky to claim her as his wife.

But even as he'd done that, he'd rebuked himself for making haste on the journey to Granada. They should have had rest days. He'd been a fool to insist they push on. Just because he and his men could endure days on end in the saddle, it didn't mean his precious wife could.

And this knowledge boosted his willpower. For his wife was naked beneath the sheet, as was he. Any other woman in his bed he'd have woken with ardent suggestions for passionate fun. But he couldn't risk it with Isabella, not when she'd collapsed from her horse. In the name of the Good Lord, she could already be carrying his heir.

A bird chirped outside, several times, then began to sing. He supposed it was a goldfinch—he always saw many of them in the palace.

They would often sit on the wall of the balcony that led from the bedchamber, pretty, little things searching for breakfast crumbs or insects amongst the flowers.

Isabella stirred at the sound floating in to the room through the vast windows shaded by thin, black muslin.

Propping up onto his elbow, he moved a strand of hair from her cheek.

Her eyes fluttered open. For a moment, she appeared disorientated, but then her attention settled on his face and she smiled. "I knew you were with me. I felt your body heat in the night."

"Were you too hot?"

"No, it is beautifully pleasant here, with the mountain breeze just sliding into the room."

Charles swiped his tongue over his bottom lip then pressed a kiss against her brow. He knew what he wanted. To lick her, all over.

"Did you eat, before you slept?" he asked.

"Yes, Luisa insisted on some bread and cheese with a few olives."

"Good. You must regain your strength. Though I hope while we are here, we'll do much resting and feasting that will nourish us both."

"And did you feast?" she asked. "With your men, when we arrived?"

"I ate a fish and bean stew and drank some, but I did not linger, for I wanted to assure myself that you were well and resting."

"I am sorry I was sleeping when you arrived. But I am glad you did join me."

"Do not apologize for a single thing." He stroked down her throat and touched the cross that sat against her skin at an angle. "For you have more color in your cheeks now, and that has pleased me so."

She smiled and gazed up at him. "I always want to please you."

He didn't answer. Instead, he very gently pushed at the sheet covering her breasts, until the first suggestions of her nipples were revealed.

She swallowed and he sensed her tensing slightly. Her eyes were wide as she looked up at him.

His cock hardened. Everything about her was so innocent and pure, yet she was willing and sensual with it.

He pulled the sheet lower, exposing her ripe breasts fully. Her skin was perfect and her nipples small, pink points. "I want you to know pleasure of every kind," he whispered as he took her right nipple between his thumb and finger. He squeezed it gently. "Will you let me show you?"

Her eyelids fluttered, as though she were concentrating on the sensation he was creating. "I will. I want you to show me."

"Good." He switched breasts, teasing the other nipple into the same stiff point. "You are so responsive." He tipped forward and kissed her, enjoying the feel of her soft, eager flesh and her slight gasp when he tugged her nipple.

But he wanted more, much more. He wanted to feast on her.

Which was exactly how he intended to start his day.

Gently, he pushed the sheet lower, past her flat abdomen, her cunny, and to her thighs. Then he broke the kiss and propped himself up to study her graceful curves. She was the perfect woman. No other compared.

"You must promise to lie still for me," he said, raising his eyebrows slightly.

"Still?"

"Yes." He raised his eyebrows. "For now, at least."

Her attention followed him as he reached across to the table on his side of the bed. Upon it was a bowl of chopped fruit—grapes, peaches, apricots—and a bowl of honey with a tiny pewter spoon in it. He placed the bowl of fruit on the bed within reach and plucked out a halved grape.

Gently, he rested it against her lips. "Eat."

She did as instructed and he watched her chew and swallow.

"And now, sweet wife, you will become my plate to dine upon." He took another grape and placed it on her sternum. He added another and another until a row of three glistening, purple spheres sat on her skin.

"Charles," she said, her breasts rising and falling with each breath. "What are you...?"

"I wish to break my fast on you." He too ate a grape, then he plucked a halved apricot from the bowl and gently set it close to her right nipple. "Stay still. I don't want the fruit to fall from where I put it."

"I'll try."

Her eagerness to please touched his heart and he kissed her again, tasting the sugariness of her lips.

He sat upright and reached for another apricot. As he placed it on her other breast, his cock twitched—he was almost at full hardness. But his pleasure would have to wait. This was about Isabella learning what her body could feel.

"You are the perfect dish," he said, stroking the undersides of her breasts in small, sweeping movements. "The perfect breakfast for an emperor."

She trembled, the apricots quivering.

"Now for some peach," he said, retrieving a segment. "Just here." He placed the soft crescent of fruit just below her navel, in the shape of a smile. "And another." He added three more, his movements slow and steady.

A trickle of juice from a peach meandered to her waist. He caught it with his finger and brought it to his mouth, sucking.

She was watching him intently.

"Here, have some." He popped a segment between her lips. "Good?"

She nodded and chewed.

"Let me try." He tipped forward and scooped the first grape he'd placed down on her sternum into his mouth. "Delicious." He kissed her. "But I'm not done yet."

"You're not?"

"Oh, no."

Outside, the goldfinches were reaching a crescendo with their music for the dawn. It calmed his eagerness to find satisfaction for both of them and he continued to slowly add peaches to her body, a pattern of segments that stopped at her neat patch of hair. "There," he said, straightening to admire his handiwork. "I think I am rather good at this." He chuckled.

She laughed too and an apricot rolled from her breast.

He caught it and replaced it. "Keep still, remember."

"Yes." Her voice was breathy…excited, almost. Certainly full of anticipation. He hoped she was remembering her wedding night climax and was hoping for more of the same, because providing that was very much his intention…but not how she was expecting it.

He reached behind himself for the pot of honey and stirred the sticky, amber liquid. "What would breakfast be without this?" he said, lifting the spoon and watching the gloopy sweetness sink back to the bowl.

She didn't answer, though she balled her fists as though preparing for the unexpected.

He smiled and held the spoon over her cunny. But he didn't let it trickle—he toiled with it, keeping the blob on the end of the spoon. "Open your legs, Isabella, but don't let the fruit topple."

She held her breath then did as he'd asked.

"More than that," he said with a smile.

Her thighs parted a little wider.

"That's it." Now he let the honey drip from the spoon, right onto the spot from which he intended to lick it.

"Oh…Charles…I…"

"Shh." He replaced the spoon and set the honey aside. He stared at her face. "There is something you should know about me."

"There is?" She swallowed. Her breaths were coming fast.

"Yes, honey is my favorite treat at breakfast. I just can't resist." He shifted down the bed, placed his hands on her inner thighs, and parted the legs further. Then he poked out his tongue and ran it over her soft feminine lips.

"Oh, dear Lord." She gasped, stabbing her fingers into his hair and sending peaches, grapes, and apricots sliding to the sheets. "Charles."

"Mmm." He looked up at her shocked face. "Perfect. Not that I've finished yet."

He closed his eyes and licked her again, through every delicate fold until he found her swollen nub. The taste of honey combined with her sensual flavor had his balls tightened with longing.

"Charles, what are you…?" She coiled forward, breathing hard and tugging at his hair.

"Do not stop me," he said, raising his eyebrows at her. "For I wish to know you this way and I wish you to feel me bringing you pleasure this way." He slid a finger to her entrance and eased in.

"Oh!" Her mouth opened in a perfect circle. "Surely…surely, this is a sin…" She closed her eyes, her eyelashes fluttering, as though she were feeling anything but sinful.

"It is not a sin, I assure you," he said, kissing her inner thigh. "Now lie back and just feel."

"Oh, help me, Lord."

He smiled and licked her cunny again, sending his finger deeper into her gripping warmth. He sought her little nub and laved it with his tongue.

Her hold tightened on his hair and she groaned, dropping back to the bed. His heart did a flip of triumph. It seemed she'd forgotten about being sinful and was doing as he'd asked—giving herself up to sensation.

He kept on going, concentrating on which action of his tongue had her groaning and yanking at his hair the most. He added another finger, deep inside her, soaked now with arousal.

And he was so erect that it hurt. Moisture leaked from his cock tip and perspiration peppered the dip of his back and his underarms. The need to sink deep into her cunny and release his seed was growing by the second. But he wanted her to find pleasure on his tongue, and it wouldn't be the first time. Because he already knew this was an act he'd do again and again. Feeling her writhe and squirm and cant her hips for more was so thrilling. Hearing her gasp and pant his name and groan from a place deep in her throat was something he'd always want more of.

"Oh…oh…" Her body stiffened, her thighs clamping against his shoulders. She stilled, as if all her concentration were on one sensation.

He didn't let up. He used his fingers like a cock, rubbing her insides as he worked her deep. He flicked her nub with his tongue, fast little tweaks that she seemed to enjoy the most.

She cried out, arousal gushing from her and her cunny pulsing around his fingers. She pushed against his face, as though needing everything he could give her and more.

He gently sucked her twitching nub into his mouth, still laving it with his tongue.

Again, she cried out, yanking at his hair then clamping his face to her grinding hips.

Heated desire scorched through his veins. He could contain himself no longer, and he pulled from her cunny and rose upward. Gripping his solid cock, he angled it at her entrance and plunged into her as he swooped down for a kiss.

She whimpered and clasped his shoulders, her knees gripping his hips.

He was out of control, he knew that, and as her hot, clenching cunny seized his cock, he released his seed. Three big pulses tore cries of pleasure from his throat.

Their kiss was frantic and lust-infused as they held each other in a place where he didn't know where he ended and she began. She filled his senses, her taste, her smell, the feel of her body surrounding his.

"Charles," she gasped, stroking his hair from his face.

He was breathing hard as he looked down at her. Her cheeks were flushed and her pupils wide.

"I never, in my imagination…thought that…"

"Would feel so good?" he said.

She laughed breathlessly. "That a man would even do that to a woman." She paused. "Or is it only emperors and empresses?"

He too laughed. "I believe it is a common bedchamber practice, though it is only emperors who dine off their wives for breakfast."

She traced his cheek to his jaw. "I am really quite sticky. Luisa will wonder what in heaven's name we have been doing."

"Breakfast in bed, that is all." He lifted slightly and felt something squishy on his chest. He glanced down. An apricot had mushed between them, its fibrous flesh totally flattened. He plucked it up and ate it. "And it has been the most delicious breakfast in which I have ever indulged."

CHAPTER EIGHT

"W HAT ARE THESE beautiful, red flowers?" Isabella asked as she stood on their private balcony. All around them were urns and vases full of blood-red bouquets. They reminded her of the sapphires her mother had worn around her neck.

"Carnations, I believe," Charles said, pouring her wine. "Do you like them?"

"They are exquisite, truly beautiful. I have never seen anything like this." She stroked one of the velvety petals, of which there were many per bloom. "They remind me that I am far from home, but at the same time I *am* home." She smiled and wondered if he understood.

"Home is a funny thing, don't you think? It can be a place, but also a person."

"I suppose that is true." She paused. "And perhaps that is how I am feeling."

Charles smiled. "Please sit." He gestured to the chair beside him. Both were in the shade, for the afternoon was warm, even though it was still early in the year and the sun low.

Isabella sat and took her wine. "Which is your favorite area of the palace?"

"It is all wondrous, though I especially like the Court of the Lions."

"Why?" She took a sip of the wine. It was sweeter than Portuguese wine and she'd discovered she enjoyed that. "Is it the lion statues around the fountain?"

"No, not really. They are small for lions, don't you think?"

"I would agree, though I have never seen a real lion."

"Neither have I. It is just that I imagine them to be big." He paused. "It is the arches and columns surrounding the fountain that I find so pleasing…so unusual in their decoration."

"They are very beautiful. Intricate and complex, too."

"And the halls within, they are untouched by Ferdinand and Isabella, which I am grateful for, as they are quite fascinating. An insight into the people before us."

"I must spend more time there," she said.

"But you liked the Hall of the Two Sisters?"

"Oh, yes." She sighed at the memory of walking into the small room and looking up. The detail was exquisite, the marble seeming to unfold in hundreds of tiny pieces down toward the domed windows. She could have stared at it for hours, not least because Charles had wound his arms around her waist and pulled her back to his chest so she could relax as she stared upward.

"So you like it here?" he asked, taking her hand. "At the Alhambra?"

"Very much so. I hope we stay a while."

"We can stay as long as we wish. This is your court now if that is what you choose."

"It is a very grand court indeed, and yes, let's stay while we can."

"We can! It is ours." He made a sweeping gesture. "And I will build you your own private palace within these walls. You only have to tell me what you desire and I will make it a reality."

She smiled, her heart seeming to overflow. "I have everything I desire because I have you."

He brought her hand to his mouth and kissed her knuckles. "It is I who has everything, more than I deserve, more than I could have ever dreamed."

She smiled and glanced away.

"What is it?"

"Nothing." She studied the tops of the mountains, unable to rid the image of her brother's face when Charles had ordered Eleanor back to Madrid, even though he'd wanted to marry their father's young widow.

"Please, I beg you tell me." He leaned forward. "I do not wish for us to have secrets."

"It is not a secret."

"So tell me."

"My brother, John."

"The king?"

She smiled. "Yes, the king. You sent Catherine to be his bride."

"Yes, and they seem to be a very good match, don't you think?"

"They *are* a good match." She hesitated and took her wine again, cupping it in both hands. "But he wanted to marry Eleanor, your eldest sister, not your youngest. I believe he wrote to you asking for her hand."

He pulled in a deep breath and set his attention on a bumblebee hovering near a flower to his left. "She was his father's widow, Isabella."

"I am aware of that. I lived in the same court." She tipped her head and studied him. It was hard to equate this Charles as the man whose refusal had slashed her brother's heart.

"But did you not think that was…strange?"

"That they marry? No, Eleanor is the same age as John. She was woefully young to be married to my father. And…"

"And?"

"They were in love. John and Eleanor. They saw only each other. Only wanted to be together."

He shook his head. "It could not be."

"It shattered his world." She poured more wine. "And I had to stand by his side and watch, helplessly."

Charles stood and walked to the balcony edge. Gripping the low wall, he stared into the distance. "I needed Eleanor back in Madrid. And Catherine... she had spent too many years with my mother. As a companion. She was a maiden, unwed and unknown to the world."

"'Unknown to the world'?"

He turned. "My sisters are very dear to me, but they are powerful in their own right, intelligent too. They understand their roles in the family. They have Habsburg blood running through their veins. They understand their duty to marry, use their education accordingly, and continue our lineage."

Isabella understood, though it was a bitter taste. "So what of Eleanor now?"

A tendon flexed in his cheek as he studied her.

"Charles?" She could tell he was reluctant to answer. "What of Eleanor now?"

"She is to marry King Francis, and now that you have given me a way to release him in a...controlled manner...that will go ahead sooner than anticipated."

Isabella's eyes widened. "And Francis has agreed?"

"Yes, it is part of the treaty I signed with him."

"Well...that is a surprise."

"To you, yes, but my brother, Ferdinand, approves. Actually, we both agree Eleanor is the perfect person to let us know if Francis is planning any more invasions or usurping."

"Your sister is to become the Queen of France and your spy." She shook her head. "I have to say it is quite brilliant if..."

"If what?"

"If Eleanor can tolerate it. I know her well, but I cannot quite decide if she will be up for the challenge or utterly repulsed."

"You will be pleased to know she is up for the challenge...at least she is now that John is married to Catherine. Before that, she was holding out hope I'd change my mind."

Isabella sighed. "I suppose as emperor, it is your prerogative to make these decisions."

"Yes. It is." He sat next to her. "But you are empress and from now on, we will make such decisions together." He paused. "Decisions that will perhaps take in the state of our people's hearts as well as the necessary politics to be addressed."

"I hope that will be the case." She pointed in the distance. "Look, an eagle."

He studied it for a moment, then said, "My grandfather, he was a wise man."

"Emperor Maximilian's reputation spread far and wide."

Charles laughed quietly. "Some things good and some bad."

She shrugged.

"He once told my father that he and my mother should wear the crown as one."

"As one?" Isabella asked.

"As one person. When my father, Philip, claimed his title as king he was doing it because he was married to the Queen of Castile."

"And it *was* his right."

"Yes, it was, but his father told him that Joanna was a well-educated and prudent woman who knew her people well and he must include her in decisions, that they must reign as one, the outside world seeing them as one power with which to be reckoned and obeyed."

"And one protector of their people."

"Naturally." He inclined his head and was quiet.

Isabella got the feeling there was more to be said.

"But he didn't do that," Charles went on. "Or he didn't get the chance to."

"I am sorry. I know you were young when he died."

"Yes, I was. My parents traveled to Spain and I never saw my father again and have only these last years been reacquainted with my mother."

"It is a good thing that you've reconnected."

He took her hand, weaving his fingers with hers, then studied their clasp. "It is. She is wise council, if a little somber... No, *a lot* somber."

"She has never recovered from her grief? The loss of her husband?"

"No. She was a feisty, fiery young woman and that hasn't changed, but now the flame burns dark—black, even—and it is true, her life has never been the same since she lost Philip. Her love must have been as soul-achingly deep as mine is for you."

She smiled gently. "His death was quick, was it not? Unexpected too. That must have made it all the harder for your mother."

He closed his eyes, sucked in a breath.

"Charles, my love. I am sorry, I..."

"The official line is he died of a swift disease, but I know differently."

"You do?"

"Yes." He banged his chest. "I believe it was Joanna's father, our shared grandfather, who poisoned him."

"But...why would Ferdinand, the King of Aragon, do such a thing?"

"For the crown, of course. He hated my father, wanted him dead so he could wear the crown in Joanna's place. He spread a rumor that my mother was *la loca* and unfit to rule and killed my father so he could be King of all Spain."

"That is a terrible injustice." Isabella paused. "And I find it hard to believe of the king. It is too terrible."

"You do not need to believe it." His voice quieted. "But we said no secrets, and that is a secret hurt and betrayal that I carry in me. I wish you to know it." A flash of vulnerability crossed over his eyes and his lips pressed together.

"Charles." Boldly, she stood then sat on his lap and pulled him into a hug. "I am so very sorry for this burden you carry."

He didn't answer, but he did wrap his arms around her and press his face into the crook of her neck.

She ran her hand through the thick strands of his hair and kissed his head. "But you are King of Spain now, in your mother's place. That must fill her with pride."

"Yes, she says it does."

"Good." She pulled back and cupped his cheeks, lifting his face to hers. "I am glad." She set a kiss over his lips, the first she had instigated since they'd married. For a second, she was hesitant, but then he opened up and stroked his tongue against hers.

He tasted of wine and mountain breeze and her body reacted to his flavor.

She kissed him a little deeper, pressing her breasts to his chest. In the distance, the eagle called.

"You lead me to temptation," he murmured onto her lips as he slid his hand to her breast and squeezed gently.

"So give in to it." She pushed against him. "I am yours."

He moaned softly and caught her mouth in a deeper kiss. It quickly heated and he gripped her around the waist, lifting her slightly. "Like this," he said. "Sit astride me."

"But I..." It seemed most indecent to sit on him as though he were a horse.

"Shh, I'll show you it will be good like this."

She did as he'd asked, her gown bunching up to her thighs, then glanced left and right.

"There is no one to see us," he said. "We ordered privacy. Everyone knows it would be a very bad day for them should they disobey."

His dark eyes sparkled up at her. They were full of desire and love.

Rocking forward, she felt the hardness in his breeches. "It must be terribly uncomfortable to have such a solid appendage. Especially when riding a horse."

He laughed. "It is not so solid all of the time, my dear Isabella." He cupped her ass over her gown. "Only when I want you, when I need to be as close to you as possible." He lowered his voice. "When I can barely think for wanting to be inside your sweet body."

"I have much to learn." Her heart rate was picking up.

"And I will teach you all of it." He peppered kisses down her neck and at the same time fumbled with breeches. "And you will enjoy every lesson."

She arched her back and gripped his shoulders, lifting her face to the sky and letting the warm breeze tousle her hair.

"I want you to sit on me," he murmured against her throat. "Lift up and sit on me."

Opening her eyes, she looked down. He held his cock in his fist, the tip deep mauve and impossibly wide.

"Just...sit? I don't think that's possible."

"It is." He slipped his free hand between her legs, disappearing in the material of her gown. "Are you wet for me?"

"I don't...oh..."

He'd found her cunny and was stroking through her soft folds. She trembled and curled her toes on the hard tiles.

"You are wet," he said with a smile, then he kissed her. "Your body wants mine, so do not fear anything."

"I don't fear it. Not with you."

"That is the right answer." Once again, he circled her waist and urged her to lift.

She felt the warm head of his cock probing her entrance.

"Oh, my love." He moaned softly and slid his fingers into her hair. "My urges are powerful, but I don't want to hurt you."

"It won't hurt. It hasn't before." As she'd spoken, she willed her tight muscles to relax and lowered onto his cock, just a little. But he was so thick and wide and she struggled to take his first inch. Luckily, her wetness eased his way and she stared into his eyes as she took him a bit more.

His pupils were dilated as he looked at her, and his body was tense, as though held under a powerful spell.

"Does that feel good for you?" she whispered against his lips. What they were doing was hidden from the world by her gown and she was glad of that, as they weren't in their bed.

"It is the best feeling in the world," he said, his voice seeming deeper than usual. "Being with you is the best feeling in the world."

"I am glad."

"Keep going, until you have taken all of me."

Slowly, she took his entire length, until her behind was touching his thighs.

"Oh, dear Lord." He moaned, clasping her buttocks, over her gown. "I could stay inside you forever."

"Now what should I do?" she murmured.

"Rock, like this." He urged her to grind her hips forward.

The moment she did, her sweet needy nub rubbed against his hard body. She gasped. "Oh...Charles."

"You like that?"

"Yes."

"It's hitting your little bud?"

"Yes..." She ground forward again. The sensation of his cock rubbing her inside and applying pressure to her nub was delicious. "Oh, that's good...yes...I understand now."

"So find your pleasure, my beautiful wife." He was watching her with wonder. "Use me to find your pleasure and then I will find mine."

"Yes...oh...yes." Again, she lifted her face to the sky and arched her back. She rode onto him, working her hips forward and backward, each grind up against him building the pressure within her. Each crush of his body excited her more.

Soon, she'd lost any inhibitions and was working herself toward release. It was there, her climax, and she wanted it.

"My love, you are so beautiful like this," he said, once again kissing her extended neck. "You make me crazy for you."

Isabella didn't answer because her breath had been stolen by the climax about to claim her. For a moment, she felt like a wild woman, held hostage by pleasure, and then it pulsed through her in torrents of bliss.

She cried out and clung to his shoulders as she rode through her pleasure. It filled her with satisfaction and journeyed to every corner of her body. "Charles…oh…yes…Charles."

"Ah…yes…" His face twisted and he closed his eyes. Surging his hips upward, he found his pleasure. "Isabella…" He gasped, clinging to her in a steely embrace. "Oh…that is…"

She clasped his face and kissed him, their hot, panting breaths tangling. Witnessing his ecstasy was as wonderful as feeling her own. It cemented her belief that they had been created solely for one another.

"I love you so much," he said. "Each day, I love you more."

"And I love you." She pushed his hair from his hot brow.

"You do?"

"Yes. Of course I do."

"That has filled me with such happiness," he said. "I hoped for affection, friendship…but love…I didn't dare hope."

"Oh, Charles. Don't you see? I was destined to be at your side— I've known that all of my life. You are the only man for me. No other can compare or would ever."

"And you are the only woman for me. There will never be another." He paused. "You have to believe that. Even when we are apart. Even if your imagination runs wild. I will only ever want and love you. I am not a man who would cheat your love or trust."

"I do know that. You show me it in every smile and kiss, dear husband of mine. I adore you and trust you with my heart and my life."

CHAPTER NINE

WEEKS TURNED INTO months and Isabella didn't want anything to change. Charles had been worth the wait and she thanked God every day for giving her the faith and the patience to commit to him when he hadn't committed to her.

But he was committed to her now, she knew that. They hardly slept at night for loving each other, and then they didn't rise from the bedchamber until noon most days. Charles kept meetings with nobles, council, and clergy brief because he preferred to be with her.

Luisa claimed to have never seen a man so smitten with his wife and when Isabella caught him watching her with a slight smile on his lips she believed it to be true.

"What is happening here?" Isabella asked one afternoon as they walked through the *Mirador de Lindaraja* garden.

"I am having new flowers planted throughout the palace," Charles said, gesturing with a sweep of his hand to the overturned soil. "Red carnations."

"Red carnations?"

"Yes, I know you love them so. It is a gift for you, so that you can visit an abundance of them should you wish."

"You are so very thoughtful." She smiled.

"In truth, I struggle to think of anything other than you." He shrugged and shook his head. "To the detriment of some of my responsibilities as emperor, I fear."

Concern gripped her. "I do not wish to distract you so much that you cannot perform your imperial duties."

"Do not worry. I have clever and intelligent noblemen to help me." He paused. "Though at some point, I will have to travel to Rome."

"You will?"

"Yes, I have been crowned Holy Roman Emperor by the electors, but until the pope places the crown upon my head, I have not secured the title for our future son. I think you'll agree it is most important that I do that so he does not have to go through the prince's election process, as I did… It was somewhat troublesome."

"I agree it is a title to which our son must have claim."

Charles sighed and looked away.

"What bothers you? The fact we do not have a son on the horizon yet?"

"No, for I know these things take time, but it also takes time for a son to grow into a man and the role of emperor is complex and requires experience."

"One not suitable for a child."

"Or even a boy on the brink of manhood. There are so many complexities within the empire, and with Martin Luther, the heretic, gaining a following and the so-called League of Cognac I must contend with thanks to Francis, who has the ears of northern Italy listening to him." He sighed. "I have power-grabbing, slick-tongued, wealthy men who seem to prod at me constantly and try to force me out of favor with the papacy with intentions of forcing me from Italy altogether."

"Oh, Charles, it is a big burden to bear."

"At least I hold Naples secure." He nodded as they walked from the garden into a courtyard with a splashing fountain. "But do not fear, my love, it is a burden I can carry. It is my destiny."

"I know that you have broad shoulders for such a weight. I also think," she said, stopping in a shady spot, "that your brother, Ferdinand, could bear it."

He frowned down at her. "What are you saying?" His tone was a little sharp.

"Why don't you name him as your successor with the provision he passes the title on to your son, not his own? That would solve the problem of needing to span a few decades, would it not?"

His frown deepened.

For a moment, Isabella wondered if she'd gone too far with her suggestion.

"The title would have been his to win had he been my elder brother, not younger." Charles nodded slowly. "It is a wise and prudent idea. Yes. I will think on it, perhaps discuss it with my Aunt Margaret, who has come to know Ferdinand well." He swept his lips over hers. "Thank you for your council."

"I wish to help in any way I can."

"You do. Every moment of every day just by breathing." He kissed the tip of her nose and pulled her close.

She giggled.

"Your Majesty." A deep male voice.

"Alvaro, good day to you," Charles said, releasing his wife. "Are they ready?"

"Yes, this way." Alvaro smiled at Isabella. "Your Majesty." He was long-limbed with a dark beard that he kept neatly trimmed and he always wore a traditional Spanish cordobés hat—a flat cap with a wide brim and a red, silk ribbon around it.

"What is it?" Isabella asked.

"Alvaro has sourced something very special for us."

"More gifts? More surprises." She laughed. "You spoil me, dear husband."

"If I gave you the moon and all the stars in the sky, it would not be enough." He kissed her hand. "But this is not the moon or the stars. Something else entirely."

"I am intrigued."

"You should be."

The enthusiasm in Charles was contagious and her heart skipped with joy as they followed Alvaro from the courtyard and down a set of stone steps toward the stables.

"We are going riding?" she asked.

"Only if you want to, but we may prefer to watch a display."

"A display? You really are being most mysterious, husband."

Alvaro entered a shaded barn and they followed.

It smelled of straw and horse tack and dust motes danced in fingers of sunlight that sneaked in through cracks in the beams.

"We must keep our voices low," Alvaro whispered.

Charles put his arm around her waist, holding her close.

"Is it something that will eat me?" she whispered.

"No, I would not endanger you," he replied quietly.

Alvaro opened a stable door and gestured for them to follow.

It was then that Isabella saw the two majestic birds sitting hoodwinked on perches.

"Oh, my, they are incredible."

Alvaro beamed, clearly pleased with himself. "This one is a gyrfalcon. Isn't it beautiful?"

Isabella stepped a little closer and studied the bigger of the two raptors. Its feathers were mainly white, though it had little, black specks on its wings that reminded her of a chessboard, one that had been set at an angle. Its hooked beak was pale yellow, as was its feet.

"He is a fierce predator," Charles said. "And has come from icy lands."

"And there he blends into the snow." She nodded. "What a treat to see such a beast." She pointed at the other bird. "And this one?"

"A peregrine falcon," Alvaro said, stroking the bird's breast with the back of his finger. "One of the fastest I have ever hunted. Almost too quick to see it stoop."

"I have heard." She was fascinated. She'd hunted falcons growing up, but these two birds were truly magnificent. "And I look forward to seeing him fly."

"We can see that now, if you'd like," Charles said.

"Oh, yes." She nodded and clasped her hands. "I cannot think of a more pleasing entertainment."

"Good." Charles nodded at Alvaro. "We will meet you at the paddock."

"Very good, Your Majesty."

Thirty minutes later, Isabella and Charles sat under the shade of a fig tree on soft, cushioned seats. A tray of wine had been set before them as well as honeyed ham and walnuts.

Isabella popped a walnut in her mouth. "Will there be mice here? For the birds to hunt?"

"Alvaro has a way to demonstrate them in action without relying on mice from the stables showing themselves."

Beside a tall wall dotted with candelabras, Alvaro stood with the birds. He had two men helping him and had just transferred the gyrfalcon to his glove. In his opposite hand, he had a length of rope with something tied onto the end of it.

One of his helpers took the hood off the bird. It roused its feathers and looked around with its beady, black eyes.

"He is quite the find," Isabella said. "A delight, for sure."

"I am glad you like him. I'd hoped you would."

"Yes, I..." Her words trailed off as Alvaro launched the bird into the air.

It took a couple of beats of its huge wings and then it was circling, gaining height.

"It's huge." She gasped. "Bigger than I could ever have imagined."

"Look, watch what's going to happen." Charles pointed at Alvaro.

He was swinging his thin rope in ever-increasing circles over his head.

"That's a chunk of meat on the end." Charles pointed. "Watch the bird try to take it."

Sure enough, the gyrfalcon spotted the food and then dived down, talons outstretched.

Alvaro snatched the food away from his reach at the last moment.

"Oh, look at that." Isabella clapped at the sight. "He didn't get it."

"He'll try again." Charles gestured to the bird, who was clearly determined as he was gaining height again and concentrating on the spinning rope. His attention didn't move from it.

Sure enough, he dived in for the kill once more.

And once again, Alvaro didn't let him catch the food.

"Oh, the poor thing must be hungry," Isabella said, hopping up and down on her seat.

"Yes, he has to be. Otherwise, there'd be no show. He'd be fed up."

"And it *is* quite the show." She grinned at her husband then quickly watched what was going on again.

Alvaro was swinging the rope with gusto now. He whistled at the bird, who had sat atop a stable. Wings folded in, head cocked. "Come get it!"

The bird took to the air, the ends of its wings like spread fingers. For a moment, it was silhouetted by the sun, then it came into perfect view as it swooped at the end of the rope.

This time, Alvaro let him get it, and the rope was downed to the dusty ground beneath the gyrfalcon's lethal claws.

"That was incredible," Isabella said. "I've hunted falcons before, but they're smaller and I've never seen such skill with a rope like that."

"I am glad you enjoyed it."

"I did." She sipped her wine. "You are such a thoughtful husband."

"I try to be." He kissed her cheek. "Do you want to watch the peregrine fly?"

She batted at a buzzing insect, then another.

"The wasps are devilish this year," Charles said, flapping his hand over the wine. "Always thirsty, always thieving."

"And I don't want another sting like last week." She rubbed her upper arm, remembering the pain.

"Come, let us go eat inside. We will watch the peregrine tomorrow." He stood and took her hand. "Thank you, Alvaro," he said with a wave. "The empress enjoyed seeing the gyrfalcon hunt very much."

Alvaro bobbed his head politely, then began to draw in the rope, the bird following the last scraps of food on the end.

Charles and Isabella hugged the edge of the courtyard as they headed toward their chambers. The shade provided protection from the sun and a benevolent mountain wind wafted through stone tubs full of delicate, white flowers, making their little blooms dance.

"The bird is so strong and powerful," Isabella said, linking arms with Charles. "With such stamina."

"Qualities your husband also has, do not forget that." He kissed her temple and laughed softly.

"How could I forget?" She spread her hand and breezed it over the flowers as they walked. "You show me often enough." She thought of the night before when he'd tossed her onto the bed straight after she'd finished bathing and pleasured her for hours, driving her to climax three times at least.

A shiver of desire went through her. Would they ever get enough of each other's bodies? She didn't think so. She only hoped that soon their passion would result in a baby.

"You smell good today," he said, moving in close as they walked.

"Luisa brought me a new soap, one made of rose petals."

"I like it…a lot."

"It is only you I want to please."

"And you do, frequently."

"Like last night?" she asked.

"Last night was incredible. It always is when we're together." His hand drifted from the small of her back to her behind and rested there.

Heat from his palm traveled through her body and her nipples tightened.

They stepped indoors, into the coolness the stone floors and tiled walls provided. Passing two uniformed guards with pikes, they entered the dining room. It was long with a domed roof and walls that had more strange writing etched into the brickwork. The table was laden with bread, fruit, cold meats, and cheese, along with five huge vases of flowers, several fat candles, and jugs of wine and water.

"It is fortunate I am hungry," Isabella said as a servant stepped past holding a tray of yet more food—fish and olives.

"I am only hungry for you," Charles said quietly as he stroked her buttocks over her gown. "It seems nothing else will satisfy me these days."

"Is that right?" She stepped up to the side of the table, plucked up a grape, and popped it into her mouth. "How hungry for me are you?" She set her concentration on him, ignoring the staff still setting the table. "I want to know." She stroked her tongue over her lips, catching a little grape juice.

"Very." His eyes were heavy, the way she'd learned they became when he was thinking of getting her naked. "More than you could ever imagine."

A thrill went through her. How easy it was for her husband's need to be stoked. She reached for another grape, chewed it slowly, then swallowed. "And are you going to satisfy that hunger?"

"Yes." He stepped up to her and circled his arms around her waist.

"When?" Her heart was thudding now, anticipation winging through her veins.

"Now." He dragged her close, his hard cock pressing into her over their clothing.

She gasped. "*Charles!*"

He reached one hand behind her and swept several plates to the floor. Pomegranates, figs, onions, and oranges scattered and rolled.

"What are you doing?" She clutched his shoulders.

"What I need to do more than I need to breathe." He caught her mouth in a passionate kiss and gripped her waist. He hoisted her upward, moving back with her.

The next thing she knew, she was seated on the table, where the food had been, and he'd stepped between her legs.

"Oh...but..." They were not alone and this was heating up fast. "Charles, I—"

His kiss was frantic as he bunched up her gown. Then suddenly, he broke away and looked around. For a second, it seemed as if the spell had been broken. But then, "Get out!" he roared. "Everyone, out. Get out now!"

There was a frenzied stampede of feet. Courtiers and staff ran past them, making for the door, accidentally kicking and trampling the fallen food as they went.

Charles didn't wait to see if he'd been obeyed—he knew he would be—and he kissed her again.

The door slammed. They were alone.

"I crave you. My cock craves you," he managed as he fumbled with his breeches. "Heaven help me, I need to get inside you."

"I crave you more." She was breathless, lust like another living feverish being within her. "Do it."

She coiled her legs around his waist and angled her hips for his cock. And he was there, hot and hard and ready.

He pulled her close again, dragging her onto his erection.

She cried out, loving the rapid entry that stretched her deliciously. "Oh...Charles."

"My love." He gripped her hair and kissed her as he started up a thumping, pounding rhythm. "Take all of me."

She groaned and kissed him back. Her cunny was fluttering around his cock and each time he pulled her onto him, her nub was compressed against his body. The need in her grew. Having him so desperate for her that he couldn't even wait for the privacy of their bedchamber was a new thrill.

"Yes," she gasped, grinding against him. "Yes, yes, like that."

He grunted a reply, sped up, and clasped her right breast.

A jug of wine fell. A goblet clattered to the floor.

She was almost there, the pressure about to overspill. Her skin prickled, and she held her breath, clutching his behind as she buried her face in his neck.

The climax was swift and hard and stole her breath. Her toes curled in her shoes and she gripped his buttocks tightly. When she did manage to drag in a breath she huffed it out in a cry of delight.

Her cunny was throbbing around his cock, her arousal slick and hot.

"My love," he gasped. "You have found pleasure?"

"Yes. Oh...yes..." She reached for him and kissed him through her gasps for breath.

But then he broke the kiss and pulled from her.

"Charles." Her eyes widened. "What are you...?" She knew he hadn't found his pleasure.

"Like this." He turned her. "Bend over the table. I want you like this."

He applied pressure between her shoulder blades and she bent forward on the cool surface. Her right hand landed on a hunk of bread. Her left in a bowl of jam.

"I want to see you like this," he said gruffly as he shoved up her gown so that her ass cheeks were exposed. "In the name of...yes...like this."

He pressed against her right foot, pushing her legs apart.

She felt so exposed, so at his mercy. In the broad light of day, over the dining table, her buttocks on show and her cunny wet and pliant. Surely, she'd have to confess this as a sin.

"You are a dream come true," he said, palming her ass cheeks. "Now get ready for me again."

She twisted to look over her left shoulder. His hair hung forward messily and his cheeks were flushed. His tunic had come undone, exposing his chest hair, and he was breathing heavily.

He angled his cock at her cunny, sliding the tip over her lips before finding her entrance and pushing in.

The new angle had her gasping and she rested her brow on the cool of the table.

"Does it feel good?" he asked, gripping her waist.

"Yes...yes...do it."

He growled then plunged deeper still.

She let out a wail of delight and arched her back. "Oh...yes..."

"I must surely...be in...heaven," he muttered, pulling almost out and slamming in again, dragging her back onto him as he thrust his hips forward.

His action jolted the entire table and milk sloshed from a bowl and a vase of flowers toppled, landing messily on a plate of cheese.

She closed her eyes and tensed. His cock was so very solid and seemed to hit a place that needed that denseness riding over it roughly. Yes, so roughly. It was good.

Fisting her hands, she expelled a breath with each of his wild lunges. The pressure was growing again, but it was different this time. It was dark and deep and thick with promise.

She recognized now when he was about to release his pleasure. His guttural gasps and bliss-infused groans and a slip of his usual fierce self-control. She let her own bliss wrap around her, pulse from her, pierce through her very soul.

He flooded her with his seed, adding to the heated wetness in her cunny, and tipped over her, his chest landing on her back as he continued to buck into her.

She squirmed and cried out, loving the spread of ecstasy that was wending through her body, over her skin and up her spine to her scalp.

The back of her neck tingled where he kissed her, where his breaths blew like a storm. She wasn't sure he'd ever been so deep inside her.

"My love," he gasped, when he eventually stilled. "Are you quite all right?"

"I am...I..." She opened her eyes and spread her sticky, jam-covered fingers. "Oh...I have never been better, despite this mess." She giggled. "Whatever will the staff think of us?"

"It does not matter." He moved her hair from her ear and kissed just below it. "For we are emperor and empress and it is our duty to produce an heir. We are just working on that."

"In all honesty, after the thrill of watching the hunt this morning and then bending over this table for my husband, I do believe we have a good chance of achieving our goal."

"I hope so, my love, but I am not against continuing to try." He moved his hips, his cock rubbing against her tender internal flesh.

She moaned softly. "I like trying," she whispered. "A lot."

CHAPTER TEN

1527
Valladolid, Spain

"I SABELLA, PLEASE, DO not worry yourself with these matters." Charles took his wife's hand in his. "I implore you."

"I am empress—how can I not worry?" She shook her head. She had lines beneath her eyes and her skin was pale. "It is my duty to worry and God will walk with me every step."

"I think, on this occasion, God would like you to hand over the burden of ruling to my shoulders."

She reached for the cup of hot water and honey she liked to have close by at all times. "Soon I will give birth and this will all be over."

His heart squeezed with fear. Every time he thought about his beloved wife going through the dangerous and painful ordeal of childbirth, the panic in him rose. How could he live if something were to happen to her? This was her first child. What if her body wasn't strong enough to cope with birthing? What if she bled, or died? Or the baby died? He could lose them both. Was there ever a scarier time in a man's life than this?

He didn't think so. He'd rather ride into battle without a weapon than face this. Rather come up against a pack of wolves when he was naked and alone in a forest. It would be considerably less terrifying.

But face it he must, and he didn't want Isabella to think he was fearful of the process. How could that help? Besides, they had created the situation. They'd wanted it. His desire for an heir was real and important. Though right now, as his wife rested her hand on her large, swollen belly and fluttered her eyes closed, exhaustion coming over her yet again, he wondered if it was worth risking her—any of it.

He would order the best surgeons and nurses. She would want for nothing, and when it was over she would rest and be pampered like no woman before her.

Quickly, he kissed the cross that sat around his neck and sent a prayer to God to look after his most precious possession at this dangerous time. He tried and failed to push down a wave of guilt that it was his seed that had put her in this position.

Isabella's ordeal started the very next day.

Charles had left her sleeping under Luisa's watchful eye and was with Alvaro discussing a letter from Ferdinand about war-torn Hungary and the threats to his brother's right to rule. The situation was complex and had become more complex for him, as emperor, only the week before. Not that he'd worried Isabella about his troops sacking Rome. He'd resisted, despite wanting her wisdom, and kept the ghastly situation under wraps, for now at least.

But he wouldn't be able to ignore it for long.

Just like he couldn't ignore the high-pitched scream of agony that echoed down the long corridor from their bedchamber.

"Oh, my Lord, have mercy." He'd been running but came to a rapid halt outside the door and stared at a knot in the wood. "What is going on in there?"

"A woman must fight hard to give birth to a child," Alvaro said, resting his hand on Charles's shoulder and also breathing fast after their run through the Pimentel Palace, the courtyards, and up the stone staircase. "But to give birth to a prince, a king and an emperor, that will require considerable strength."

Charles buried his face in his hands as another almighty scream bellowed through the door. His guts twisted and he screwed up his eyes. The sound was bloodcurdling. Pure torment. How could he have done this to her?

"Sit," Alvaro said. "There is nothing you can do but pray."

Charles allowed his most favored courtier, confidant, and friend to steer him to a polished, wooden bench. He sat heavily and then sipped from the goblet of strong wine that was placed in his hand by a member of staff. "I have prayed for her to give birth easily and quickly every day from the moment she told me she was pregnant." He shook his head. Had his prayers been unheard?

"Have faith. Your prayers will be answered."

"It doesn't sound like it." Charles stared at the door as another scream hollered out.

Alvaro didn't answer.

Charles took a few big gulps of wine. He had to try to distract himself. "I am greatly embarrassed by the imperial troops, Alvaro. Their behavior in Rome has made me look powerless. And now they hold Pope Clement hostage. It is a situation only the devil must have thought up for me."

Alvaro shook his head and poured them each more wine.

"What are you thinking, Alvaro?"

"Your Majesty, you expressed a keen desire to have your audience with the pope. Perhaps your troops have purposely hastened that meeting for you."

"Taken it into their own hands." Charles glanced at the bedchamber door. All was quiet...for now. "That may be, but their pillaging and brutal actions are unforgivable."

"Men need paying."

Charles's scowl deepened and he forced himself to think of matters of the empire rather than what his wife was going through—that was too scary. "The wayward troops have done a great disservice to God and the Catholic Church. The heretics will say it is a chink in our armor, a crack in loyalty. King Henry of England will be laughing at me."

Suddenly, the bedroom door burst open. A young maid ran out holding an empty pail.

"What is it?" Charles jumped up and rushed to her.

"We need more water to warm over the fire."

"I will get it." He grabbed the bucket and ran down the corridor. At least this was one thing he could do for Isabella.

When he returned at speed, all thoughts of the ransacking, and Pope Clement, and his enemies had left his mind.

The bedchamber was quiet and that was ominous. It was infinitely worse than the screaming.

"How is she?" he asked at the door as he passed in the water.

"Her Majesty is tired," the young maid, said shaking her head. "The babe is exhausting her."

A new rush of terror went through him. "Can she not deliver? Is she going to die?"

"Dona, bring that water here." A stern, older female voice came from the room.

"Your Majesty." Alvaro was at his side. "Let the women do their work."

"Dona!"

"Save her," Charles said to the maid and pointed into the room. "Do not let her die. Do not let her die. Save my wife, your empress. Save her!"

"Yes, Your Majesty." The maid bobbed politely then shut the door in his face.

It nearly broke his nose.

"They are doing all they can," Alvaro said. "We should pray your wife's suffering is soon over and she holds your healthy son in her arms."

"Yes." The whirlwind of emotions blustering through Charles were almost too much to handle. He was frightened but felt helpless to do anything about it. And he wasn't fearful for himself—it was for his wife and child, or was it? Because he needed her so much, it was like his need for air. He wanted to start and end each day with her for the rest of his life and he'd taken to praying that he'd die first so he didn't have to live without her—so he didn't turn into his mother, a grief-racked shadow of herself waiting for a reunion in heaven.

A long, low moan rumbled through the door. He heard excited shouts of encouragement, a woman imploring Isabella to keep going—Luisa's voice, he thought. And then all went quiet. It was as if the world had stopped moving and the clocks had stopped ticking.

"Holy Father, please…" He steepled his hands beneath his chin and closed his eyes.

Alvaro squeezed his shoulder.

Charles held his breath.

Then he heard it. For a moment, he wasn't sure if he was dreaming, if he heard it because he wanted to so badly. But no, it was definitely there. An infant's indignant cry filled the air. It was the happiest sound he'd ever heard.

And he couldn't help himself. He pushed into the room, desperate to check on his wife's condition. It was instinctive, a primitive urge. One that couldn't be contained.

She lay on the bed, her modesty covered with a sheet stained with smears of blood, and her head lifted watching Luisa wrap the baby.

"My love." He rushed to her. "Tell me you are unharmed, I beg you."

She saw him and her expression softened. She held out her hand to him. "I am unharmed. Exhausted and bruised, but I have breath in my lungs and my heart beats."

"Thanks be to the Lord." He kissed her damp brow and pushed her hair back from her hot cheeks. "I could not have paced for much longer before my boots wore out."

"Your torment sounds preferable to mine." She raised one eyebrow, the way she sometimes did when he said something she thought foolish.

He chuckled, but the noise faded in his throat as the babe was placed in Isabella's waiting arms.

"Your son, Emperor, a healthy baby boy."

"My son." Had he ever known such joy? Such pride? His son was perfect, from his little, round face; toothless gums; and screwed-up eyes to his chubby arms and tiny feet. "Isabella." He kissed her again then touched the child's cheek. "We have a son. You have given your people a new emperor."

"God has indeed blessed us." She smiled up at him. "What shall we call him?"

"I would like to name him after my father. Philip. He would have loved to have met his grandson, the future Holy Roman Emperor."

"Philip." She nodded.

"Is that an agreement?"

"Yes, my love, if that is what you wish. His name is Philip." She kissed the tip of the child's nose. "My son, who will take Spain and Portugal into a new golden age."

"And beyond."

"Yes, he will fight the heretics and the Ottomans for Christ's glory."

"A heavy weight for a babe in arms only minutes old," Luisa said, fussing with sheets. "But let me be the first to offer you my sincere congratulations."

"Thank you," Charles said. He looked at the older woman in the room, the person in whom he'd put absolute trust, because of her local reputation, to help his wife.

"She was strong, Your Majesty," the nurse said. "He is a big child, a child with attitude." She smiled, though her voice was stern. "Your wife will need the help of Luisa and Dona over the coming weeks and months. I suggest you let her rest and feed the child under their guidance."

"Shall I hire you a wet nurse?" he asked the question again, even though he knew what the answer would be.

"No." Isabella adjusted the baby's swaddling. "I am his mother and I am utterly devoted to providing everything he needs."

"As I am to you both." Again, he kissed his wife's head, closing his eyes and lingering as he sent a prayer of thanks. "I love you. I will visit you again later."

"I would like that." She looked up at him and in her eyes he saw a new love. A love that was not just for him, but also for their son. In that moment, he knew that had his destiny not been Holy Roman Emperor, he still would have always been destined to be with Isabella. She was the only woman for him and Philip was the son of whom he'd dreamed and for whom he'd waited.

He walked from the room with his head held high. How proud he would be telling his noblemen, the bishops, his enemies and doubters that he had a son. A strong son who would wear the imperial crown one day. A son who would defend God and the word of Christ with a Spanish armada if necessary.

He would write to his Aunt Margaret at once and tell her the good news. He'd use his fastest envoy. He'd let Ferdinand, baby Philip's uncle, know of his arrival, and then he'd make a trip to see his mother, let her know that she had a grandson whose life would be spent defending her devout faith. Maybe she would even smile at the thought. Perhaps she would like to see him.

Yes. He was sure Joanna would want a visit with her grandson. How long would it be until mother and babe could travel, he wasn't sure.

He left the bedchamber and bumped straight into Alvaro, who was loitering close to the door.

"Your Majesty," Alvaro said, stepping back. "I humbly apologize." His face was pale and he gnawed on his bottom lip.

"Do not apologize," Charles said, clapping. "This is a joyous day indeed, one that requires great celebration."

"It is?" Alvaro gave a tentative smile.

"Yes!" Charles laughed at his friend's nervous expression. "All is well and I have a son. We have a son, Isabella and I. And Spain has its new king. The empire its new emperor."

"All is well...a son." Alvaro's shoulders seemed to sag with relief. "I am so pleased for you. Congratulations."

Charles pulled him into a tight hug and slapped his shoulders several times. "Thank you. Thank you. I am the happiest man in the world."

"As you should be."

Charles pulled back and his expression fell serious. "And the most relieved, I won't lie. Those screams were awful."

Alvaro nodded.

"And I thank you for keeping me company, my friend."

"It is my born duty to serve you."

"Yet one more thing for which I am grateful on this most auspicious day." He gestured at the long corridor. "Though right now, while mother and baby regain strength, we have political matters of great import to address."

"This is true."

"And letters to write."

"I will help in any way I can, Your Majesty."

They set off down the corridor together. Charles felt like he was floating, such was his joy. Memories of Isabella's tormented screams faded, and in their place came an image of her holding their tiny, perfect son.

What a blessed man he was.

CHAPTER ELEVEN

1528

"CHARLES, WHAT ARE you doing?" Isabella stared wide-eyed at the scene before her.

"He likes strawberries." Charles placed another in Philip's chubby, little hand. "Don't you, my little prince? You love them."

Little Philip sat on a blanket in the palace gardens and grasped the fruit, squeezing it between his fingers. "Bababa," he said. That was his favorite word at present and he applied it to anything and everything.

"The mess." Isabella couldn't help but smile, despite the fact that all surfaces were stained red. Philip's little, white outfit; the blanket; Charles's tunic; both of their faces.

She sat next to them, lowering herself carefully, as her belly was swollen once more. "Come here." She turned Charles to face her and swiped a sticky smear of strawberry from his chin. "Did I ever see such a messy emperor?"

He laughed. "I think you probably have, dear empress."

She giggled. "It is just as well only I see you in this state and it is not an image printed and distributed. You would lose your reputation as a serious and model Christian."

"Because I like strawberries?" He raised his eyebrows and passed another to Philip. "God created strawberries for us to enjoy, didn't he, Philip?"

Philip took the berry happily, waving it in the air and babbling at it.

"That is true." She made an attempt at wiping Philip's chin, but it was so smeared with juice, she gave up.

"Here, have one." Charles popped a berry into her mouth.

The sweet juice spread on her tongue like sunshine.

"My second son will also like strawberries." Charles smiled and swept a kiss over her lips. He then ducked and set one on her belly, not seeming to care that he might stain her gown.

But nothing could bother her on such a blissful day. "I think you are right." She sighed and held her face to the blue sky. "I like it here in Valladolid."

"Yes, it is a good base for us. You will have this child here."

"As long as I have Luisa and Dona with me, that is all I need."

"They will be. And the finest surgeon on standby."

"Birthing is women's business. The local midwife will give me the most experienced care."

"Then that is what you will have."

Philip waved his hand. "Bababa."

"Here you are, son." Charles offered him another strawberry.

He took it and squeezed it before licking the flesh from his fingers.

Isabella shook her head and smiled.

Charles stood and stretched his hands over his head. His tunic lifted, flashing the strip of hair between his navel and breeches.

A little flutter of interest caught in her belly. Despite being with child, the desire for her husband hadn't waned. He, however, was cautious about causing undue harm and had taken to sleeping in a different chamber.

Alvaro suddenly appeared on the lawn, his long legs striding from an archway in the courtyard.

"I get the feeling my sense of peace is about to be shattered." Charles dropped his hands to his sides.

Alvaro nodded at Charles, then dipped his head toward Isabella.

"What do you have?" Charles asked, holding out his hand for the scroll Alvaro held.

"News from Naples."

"Naples?" Charles snatched the scroll and quickly unfurled it. He read it, running his fingers into his hair and pulling at the strands as he did so.

"What is it?" Isabella asked, passing Philip his drink.

"That no-good, deceitful, lying king." He threw the scroll to one side and thumped one fist into the other. He then stalked to the wall and rested his palms against it, his head dropped to stare at the ground. Tension seemed to vibrate from him.

"Charles." Isabella went to stand. It wasn't easy with a large belly.

Alvaro was suddenly there, holding out his hand. "Your Majesty."

"Thank you." She allowed him to help her onto her feet. "Charles, what is in the scroll?" She looked at Alvaro.

He shook his head. He was none the wiser.

"Can you find Dona to watch Philip, please?" Isabella asked Alvaro.

"Yes, Your Majesty." Alvaro turned and disappeared once more.

"What is it, my love?" She set her hand between Charles's shoulder blades. "Please tell me and let me share the burden."

"You have enough burden with the babe in your belly. You do not need more to carry."

She ducked her head to look at his face. "I am your empress. God has made me strong enough to carry this load."

Snatching his hands away from the wall, he straightened. "King Francis, he has broken our treaty." He made a low, growling sound and kicked at a stone. It hit the wall with a thud. "Despite me still holding his sons."

Isabella was glad that Dona had appeared and scooped her sticky charge into her arms. Normally, Dona would comment on the mess, but today, she took the giggling child quickly from the courtyard.

"Does he not care what I will do to him for this?" Charles shouted. "What I will do to his family and his people?" He crashed his right fist into his left palm.

She rested her hand on his upper arm. The strain in him was palpable. "What does the message say?"

"He has invaded by land and by sea. An army and a fleet, surrounding Naples, blockading Naples...Naples...which is *mine*." He jabbed at his chest. "It is within my empire, it is my right to rule, and it is my right to pass onto my son." He glanced at the empty blanket. "Where is he? Where is our son?"

"Dona took him."

His brain seemed to switch straight back to the matter at hand. "The fleet is being run by Filippino Doria. His uncle is Andrea Doria, ruler of Genoa." He shook his head. "We are back at the start of our game of bloody chess. Francis will have the ear of the pope, and my empire will diminish."

"You do not have an eye into the future." Isabella was determined to stay calm. "I agree a siege is not good and—"

"*Not good*? It is a disaster! No food in or out of the city. A total cessation of the movement of trade and supplies."

"Which you yourself have endured before, have you not? In Pavia."

He was quiet for a moment then nodded. "Yes."

"So stay calm, for you always do."

"In public, yes." He banged his chest. "But the passion in here burns. I will not be defeated."

"I know you won't be." She took his hand, brought it to her lips, and kissed the ring that sat on his finger. "But exert some of your famed patience. Fate will throw moves your way, which you'll be able to play to your advantage." She paused. "Perhaps you'll be able to make a deal with Doria and persuade him to switch sides. Maybe fire, or flood, or plague will strike the army."

He pulled in a deep breath and closed his eyes.

"Francis is playing boldly, as you said, foolishly too. He doesn't have the stomach for a long campaign, I am sure of it. He has no idea what we could do to his sons in that time."

His face twisted and he cupped her cheeks. "My love, you are wise council and I will pray you are right."

"I will pray also. But other than that, there is little you can do to-day. We must be thankful that you are not in Naples, for that would make it an even bigger prize for Francis."

"That is true. I am glad to be here, at home, with my family."

"And we are glad to have you." She kissed him and pressed up close. "Shall we go for a siesta?"

"A siesta?"

"A naked siesta?" She slid her hand to his behind and squeezed. She loved how like a peach it was even through his breeches.

"You know how I worry." His eyebrows drew close. "About hurting you."

"You won't."

"But that doesn't stop me from worrying." He pulled back and ran his hand over her belly. "Our child is too precious, even if it is a girl."

"You know…" she said, also running her hand over her stomach. "I think I would like this one to be a girl."

He said nothing.

"My parents loved me, even though I didn't have a…you know…down there. And they had John already, so daughters were a blessing."

"You are a blessing to the entire world." He stroked her cheek. "And yes, you are right. I wish for nothing more than my wife to birth safely and my child to be healthy. Lord above, that is my heart's desire."

"And to win back Naples."

"Yes, and that." He managed a smile. "I must organize for the

Cortes and council to meet. My advisors must join us and I need to send word to your brother, King John. There is much to attend to."

"And can you have any council meetings today?" She tipped her head questioningly.

"No…I…" He looked around. "Alvaro!"

"Yes, Your Majesty?" Alvaro appeared the way he always did when Charles called for him.

"Naples is under siege, from the French. I need my noblemen and council to meet…tomorrow…and I need to have that scroll"—he pointed to the crumpled wad on the floor—"copied and sent to King John of Portugal."

"Yes, Your Majesty." Alvaro snatched up the scroll. "Anything else?"

"Yes." Charles frowned. "When you have done that I want you to sit and think also about the situation. Work out how long the city can survive. For I need your council too. You are a most trusted friend, Alvaro."

"My loyalty is to the empire." Alvaro bowed low. "And to you, Your Majesty. Your desire is my instruction." He straightened and checked that his hat was secure. "Now if you will excuse me, I will get to my tasks."

Charles nodded.

For a moment, the tranquility of the courtyard made itself known again. A family of sparrows flitted from an olive tree to a rooftop. A butterfly fluttered around a pot of pink roses and the sound of the fountain seemed to spread a sense of peace over everything.

"Come, walk with me," Isabella said softly. "You have energy in your legs that must be used up."

"I was very relaxed and calm." He held out his arm. "Until that delivery rudely interrupted our day."

Isabella took his arm. "As was I, but we can be at peace again. There is nothing to be done until tomorrow."

"That is true."

"So let the situation incubate." She touched her belly. "Let your thoughts be pregnant and then the solution will come with time."

"I have no right to claim you as mine—you are so wise and sensible." He kissed her temple as they walked.

"You are the only man by whom I could or would ever be claimed, my love."

He released a low sigh and they walked slowly in the shade.

Having been together for so long now, she could sense him settling into quiet contemplation. The cogs of his mind turning, connecting, working out the various end results and how to get the one he wanted.

The corridors of the palace were empty, everyone either in siesta or getting on with quiet tasks.

Eventually, they came to a grand room with golden gilded walls that held huge paintings of landscapes and portraits. A long table in the center was used for meetings, the soft, high-backed chairs surrounding it blue velvet and studded with silver nails.

At the head of the room was a raised section containing two more blue, velvet, throne-like chairs. These were substantially bigger, grander too with ornate woodwork and embroidered cushions with gold and silver threads depicting the Habsburg crest.

They stepped in to the quiet stillness and Isabella shut the door behind them.

"I think well in this big room," Charles said, running his finger over the backs of the chairs as he walked parallel to the table.

"As do I." She looked at a landscape painting of a river running through a valley surrounded by mountains and olive groves. "It feels as though the knowledge and wisdom of our ancestors remains in the walls."

"Yes." He smiled. "I know what you mean."

She took a grape from a bowl on the table and popped it into her mouth.

"I am sure," he said, stepping onto the plinth and removing the red, silk scarf that had been loosely tied around his neck, "that sitting here will give me some clarity."

He sat and curled his hands over the arms of the chair, resting his head back and closing his eyes. The scarf sat curled on his lap.

Isabella walked toward him, her footsteps soft. She sent thanks for her good fortune in life. Her husband was so handsome, so astute, and so calm in the face of invasion. Yes, it had angered him initially, but now he was approaching the situation with his usual grace and dignity.

She went up onto the raised section and stood before him, sweeping her eyes over his body. She wanted him the way she always did and him withholding due to his concerns for the baby was getting beyond frustrating.

And if it was frustrating for *her*, she knew it would have been driving him crazy.

His tunic was undone at several buttons and the base was rucked up, once again showing a patch of his body hair. Her attention dipped lower, to his soft scarf covering the folds of material at his groin.

A flutter of desire caught in her belly. The need for intimacy squeezed at her heart.

Stepping up to him, she folded to her knees and set her hands on his thighs.

He opened his eyes and looked at her.

"If you won't come to my bed, at least let me show you how much I love you."

"I know that you love me."

She ran her hands up his legs to his groin then took hold of the scarf and held it up. She dropped it to the floor, where it settled silently.

His eyes grew heavy.

She brushed her fingertips over the bulge of flesh behind the material.

He blew out a breath. "Isabella?"

"Let everything go from your mind, just for a few minutes, Emperor," she whispered, pulling at his breeches. "This won't hurt the baby. So relax and let me love you this way."

"Here? Now?"

"Yes, here and now. We will not be disturbed."

"Let us hope not." His fingers gripped the arms of his throne tighter.

Keeping his eye contact, she pulled out his cock. It wasn't solid, but as she held it, the flesh grew thicker.

His chest rose as he filled his chest.

"You like me touching you?"

"You know I do." His voice was a little deeper now, huskier too.

"Like this?" She ran her hand up to the tip of his erection and slipped her thumb over his slit.

"Mmm, like that."

She smiled then tipped forward and used her tongue to trace where her thumb had just been.

He bit on his bottom lip and his cock twitched within her grip.

"I love the taste of you," she murmured.

"As I do you."

Concentrating, she worked his cock from tip to root and back up again. Slowly, so slowly, feeling every thick tendon and vein.

His thighs flopped open a little, as though relaxing into her touch.

A feeling of triumph went through her. No longer was he thinking of the invasion or the siege. She had his complete and utter attention.

"Do you want my mouth?" she asked with a little smile.

He nodded. "Yes."

"So ask for it."

His eyelids fluttered closed as she twisted her grip at the top of his cock, just the way he liked.

"Ask nicely," she said, flying high on her moment of power over him.

"Empress, my love..." He gasped. "Please, take me into your sweet mouth."

She licked her lips. Her heart was beating fast, and she leaned up to hover her mouth over his tip.

She stroked her tongue around the flare of his glans.

"Ah, Isabella." He groaned, sliding one hand to her head and knocking her headdress to the floor. "Yes, like that...no...give me more." His fingers dug into the strands of her hair.

"Emperor, allow yourself to be at your wife's mercy, just for a little while."

He was breathing hard as he nodded. "You make me *loco* with need for your touch."

Which was exactly her intention. "You mean this touch?" She ran her fist to his root and squeezed gently.

"Oh, in heaven's name...please...more..."

The desperation in his voice was music to her ears. "You mean this?" She tipped forward and opened her mouth around his cock tip, taking him between her lips.

Her hair roots pulled as his grip tightened. He let out a long, low groan.

Cupping her tongue, she dropped lower onto him, taking his length into her mouth and hugging it into her warmth.

His thighs pressed against her and he moaned softly. "So good."

Isabella knew what he needed next and she pulled up again, only to drop back down, taking him as deep as she could, to the back of her throat.

He tensed and shifted his hips. The wooden throne creaked.

She pulled up, dipped down, repeated it over and over.

His moans grew more guttural, echoing around the grand room, and his hands followed the movements of her head.

"Oh...I'm...getting close..." He gasped.

She knew he was. His cock was as hard as it ever got and a slick of salty moisture coated her tongue. If she weren't already with child, he'd have entered her cunny at this stage, but today, that wasn't of concern.

"Isabella...I...oh..." He canted his hips to meet her mouth, an urgency taking over him.

She closed her eyes, a tear slipping from one of them. He was going so deep, so fast. But far from being unpleasant, it was thrilling and she tightened her lips around his solid shaft.

With a cry, he found his release, flooding her mouth.

She swallowed what he gave her, though some leaked out and she used it as lube on his shaft.

Again, his cock pulsed. His cry turned into a bliss-soaked groan and he released the tension on her hair.

She breathed deeply, pulling up and then sliding down again.

"My love." He gasped, gripping her underarms. "Oh, that was so...good."

She lifted and let his cock fall into her palm, holding it tenderly. "It was my intention to please you."

"Then you succeeded." He grinned. A sheen of sweat sat on his brow and he was breathing fast. "Please, come here."

Lifting up, she quickly found herself sitting on his lap.

"Do you think you are the first to be pleasured upon this throne?" she asked, looping her arms around his neck.

"I am not sure our ancestors were so devilish."

"You think that was devilish?" She raised her eyebrows at him.

"Devilishly good." He chuckled. "But not something I will be confessing because as I told you once before, what happens between a man and his wife is for their knowledge only."

He kissed her, a lovely, deep, warm kiss that told her how much he loved her and needed her.

CHAPTER TWELVE

1529

"MY LOVE, I don't want to go, but I have to."

"I know." Isabella turned from her husband, hugging her tiny daughter close. She didn't want him to see the tears in her eyes.

"Momma." Philip looked up at her with large, blue eyes. "Momma, can we go and play in the courtyard?"

"Dona, please, could you take Philip?"

"Yes, Your Majesty." Dona scooped up Philip and kissed his cheek. "Come with me. Let's count the butterflies. There are so many today on the flowers."

Philip nodded enthusiastically and wrapped his arms around Dona's neck. "Butterfly. Butterfly."

Isabella watched them leave the room and blinked rapidly. She had to stay strong. She was empress. Of course her husband would have to leave to attend to important business. She had agreed to this when she'd married an emperor. But leaving with *this* on the agenda? She would rather he'd been heading to Naples mid-siege. But this! This! It was foolhardy at best, suicidal at worst.

"Let me put Maria in her basket," Charles said, tenderly taking the sleeping child from Isabella's arms.

"Don't wake her," Isabella said stiffly. "I have spent many minutes getting her to sleep."

"I won't wake her," he said softly, a direct contrast to her icy tone.

Isabella watched as he cradled his daughter in his big arms and her heart softened, only to harden again at the thought of this being one of the last times he embraced Maria.

Tenderly, he laid the infant down, being careful not to let her lie on a crease. He stroked a few strands of hair from her brow, kissed her cheek, then stood and studied his daughter for a moment as though checking for signs of her waking.

"Come," he said, taking Isabella's hand and leading her onto the balcony. "We need to talk."

"I believe you said everything you wanted to say at dinner last night." Her jaw was tense, her stomach a tight ball of fear and frustration.

He sighed. "That may be, so you talk, Isabella. Tell me what you think."

"You know what I think." She gripped the wall and looked down into the courtyard, waiting for Dona and Philip to appear. A fountain splashed in the center, and pots of topiary stood in neat borders around it.

She clamped her lips together.

"Isabella." Charles stood next to her. But he didn't look at the courtyard. He stood with his back to it, his behind on the wall, and his arms crossed. "You know the terrible troubles the empire has had in Italy, and my need to be crowned by the pope is becoming ever more urgent."

She swallowed tightly. "Yes. I know that."

"The siege of Naples took its toll on relations. You know it did. I need to secure my allies."

"You have Andrea Doria negotiating and consulting on your behalf now."

"It is true, he has been a great asset since he switched allegiance from France to the empire."

"And you and Pope Clement have your treaty now. Surely, that counts for something."

"Of course it does. It gives me a window of opportunity of which I must take advantage." He paused. "And it is my vehement wish and goal to bring peace to Italy and repel the Turkish Ottoman advances."

"Quite the task for one man."

"It is not for one man alone. But I need to be there, to support Ferdinand, to delegate, to show strength. I need to go to Naples."

"Stop this talk of Naples! It is no longer a problem and it is under imperial rule." She shook her head and closed her eyes. They were going around in circles and avoiding the one thing that truly annoyed and scared her. She took a deep breath. "It is the hatred that simmers between you and Francis I find hard to bear. It shreds at my heart like a scythe through wheat."

"It is entirely his fault! This feud is all his fault," Charles snapped. "And you know it."

"This constant hostility is the fault of you both, as is this ridiculous idea for a duel." She clenched her fists in frustration. "The losses at Pavia were devastating for the French. So many noblemen died or were captured. And then you kept him prisoner, in what conditions, I do not know, for he almost died of a terrible fever. Then he has to withdraw from Naples like a dog with his tail between his legs. No wonder this hate is like a cauldron bubbling between you." She threw up her arms. "And you still have his sons held hostage. How can you not take some of the responsibility for the dispute?"

"His sons! That was *your* idea!" He pushed away from the balcony wall and turned to her, eyes wide, hands held out, palms up. "In heaven's name, it was your suggestion, Isabella."

"But I didn't know you would have them for so long. And what good has it done anyway? He doesn't care about them, his own sons, his heir. He has gone about his invasions and sieges as if they do not exist. His own flesh and blood."

"I could have had their heads chopped off, but I didn't. Perhaps he knows that I couldn't do such a thing to children." Charles frowned. "And what is more, I don't want those two boys spending all of their young lives in captivity."

"Kept like animals." She stepped away from him, stalking to the end of the balcony that gave a view over the town's orange roofs and then down into the lush valley. A honeysuckle climbing the wall next to her was alive with tiny, hovering bees. She couldn't see the beauty in anything, though. She was too angry.

"They are not being kept like animals," Charles said. "They have a highly regarded tutor and are taken out hunting. Not the case for many political prisoners, I'd wager."

She didn't answer.

"So a duel between the King of France and I is the only option," he went on forcefully. "Once I have been to Italy and secured the imperial title for our son, I will visit Francis and we will finish this once and for all. There will be one victor with no more Christian blood spilled in battles and wars. Either Francis will live or I will live. Either Francis will die or I will die. Then that will be the end of the matter."

Her heart squeezed. She'd hated those words the first time he'd uttered them. Now, in the harsh light of day, they were even worse. "What about *your* Christian blood?" She pressed her hand over her chest. "My husband's Christian blood, the emperor's Christian blood. Have you thought of that? If Francis defeats you in a duel and you die...then what? What will be left?"

"Ferdinand will rule in my place until Philip can take over." He set his jaw obstinately and stared at her.

Frustration gripped Isabella. Why couldn't he see how futile this was? How wasteful of his life, of her life, that he was potentially robbing their children of a father. "Charles!" she shouted. "When did you turn so utterly reckless?" She stomped up to him and looked up at his steely face. "Tell me. Tell me now."

"It is not reckless it is of sound judgment."

"It is not *of sound judgment*." She banged her fist on his tunic, over his heart. "It is not. And you know it, in here. Where is the calm, considered man I knew so well but has now vanished?"

His frown deepened, but he didn't move. "You cannot change my mind."

"You have to see sense." Tears pricked her eyes. "You have to see it from my perspective. I love you. I know you must go away, but not to die. Don't leave me to die of sadness."

"I won't die. I will defeat him. Have faith."

"Husband, my faith is as strong as a person's faith can be...but this." She shook her head. "Don't do it."

"The challenge has been sent by envoy." His lips tightened. "To Francis himself and to the French Ambassador. I told him, 'Had your king kept his word, we should have been spared this. It would be better for us two to fight out this quarrel hand to hand than to shed so much Christian blood.'"

"What? When? When did you send such letters?"

"This morning."

"No." She thumped his chest, then again and again. Soon, her fists were raining down on his tunic and her heart was breaking at the thought of losing him.

He stood his ground, taking what she had to give.

Tears rolled down her cheeks. Her throat tightened with sobs. "You royal fool." She gasped, banging him harder still. "Why would you do this? You are emperor. You have so many options at your disposal. You are emperor."

Her spine seemed to crumble and her knees weakened. Her mind was full of awful images of him bleeding onto the ground, the French soil drinking him up greedily.

"Isabella." He dragged her close, holding her. "You are stronger than this."

"No, no, you are wrong." She held his face in her hot palms and stared into his eyes. "Without you on God's Earth, I don't know how to be strong. I need you, Charles. I need you."

He used the back of his thumb to wipe away her tears. "You can be strong, for our children."

"They are *your* children too. They need their father."

"Have I not done my bit?"

"No...how can you say that? Philip needs you to teach him how to rule, how to be a good and pious man. Maria needs you to protect her, to help her find a marriage that isn't just for political gain, but for happiness. And..." Her words trailed off and she closed her eyes, sobs taking over. "And..."

"Shh, my love, I beg you." He rocked her in his arms. "I love you so much. I hate to see you cry."

His affection made her sob all the more. His loss would devastate her. Steal the breath from her lungs and the beat from her heart. How could he do this?

"I promise to come back to you," he said.

"How can you promise such a thing?" She sniffed. "You can't...so don't."

"I will return."

"When?"

He closed his eyes and sucked in a breath. "That, I cannot say."

She turned away from him and pressed her hand to her belly.

"Isabella. Are you unwell?"

"I believe I am with child again."

"My love." He was behind her, close. "That is wonderful news."

"You may never get to see him."

"Please. I beg you." He set his hands on her shoulders. "Do not say such a thing."

"If you cannot tell me when you will be back...if at all, then yes, I can say it. It is my right to say such a thing."

CHARLES LEFT TWO days later.

Isabella spent the next three days with her cheeks tear-stained and unable to eat or sleep. It was as though she were sitting on the edge of a cliff, feet hanging over the edge. The only thing that kept her from jumping was her children's sweet faces and their tiny bodies cuddled up to her at night.

But then on the fourth day, she woke early and walked out onto the balcony. She stood by the honeysuckle and stared into the distance. This time, she saw clearly what was there.

A huge bird of prey circled. For a moment, she wondered if it was a gyrfalcon, but then that thought shifted and in its place something else began to grow.

An idea. A potential solution. A cunning plan.

She rushed back inside and into her private solar, leaving Dona with the children.

Could she do it? Should she do it?

She clasped her hands beneath her chin and sank to her knees. "Heavenly Father, give me guidance, give me strength, for I do this for the sake of the emperor, your eternal and faithful servant. The King of Christendom." She steadied her breathing. "In the name of your Son, Jesus Christ, I do this with the best of intentions and the hope of preventing sorrow, pain, and the spilling of blood. Amen."

Standing, she straightened her gown, sucked in a deep breath, then sat at her desk. She withdrew two scrolls and uncurled the first. After dipping her quill, she began to write and she did not stop until two letters were complete. One, she addressed to her husband's aunt, Archduchess Margaret of Austria, and the other to Louise de Savoy, the mother of King Francis I of France.

Carefully, she sealed them with hot wax then applied her stamp.

Who better than to sort out this ridiculous situation than two mothers—for Margaret was like a mother to Charles.

Neither woman would want the duel. They'd see it for what it was. Bravado. Bluster. Swagger. Daring. Foolishness.

If anyone could stop it, it would be these two powerful ladies who had sway, persuasion, intelligence, and now a common enemy…the duel.

Isabella rang for a servant. She'd get the letters sent by envoy this very day. There was no point in delaying, for she might change her mind about sending them. Or Charles would get to France much earlier than expected and the letters would arrive too late.

No. They needed to be on horseback within the hour and heading north. It was her only hope, the only option that didn't have only half a chance of success.

CHAPTER THIRTEEN

A KNOCK AT the library door had Isabella setting her Bible aside. She was glad of the intrusion, if she were honest. She'd felt weary all day. "Come in."

It opened and Alvaro appeared in his usual dark clothing and black hat. "Your Majesty, I have a letter for you."

"From whom?" She received many letters, but she only really got excited if one came from Charles.

Alvaro studied the seal. "I believe it is from the Archduchess Margaret of Austria."

"It is?" Isabella sat forward, though it was getting uncomfortable to do so at six months pregnant. "I had started to give up hope of hearing from her."

Alvaro smiled and shut the door. "I am pleased also and pray it contains good news."

"Me too." She kissed the cross that sat around her neck.

"Would you like me to open it for you?"

"Yes, please." She gestured to the chair next to her. "And read it if you would." She paused and smiled. "It will save me from having to relay it to you after I have perused it." She picked up a cup of honeyed tea and sipped. But it was hard to contain her anticipation. Would she be scolded for meddling or would Margaret have news?

Alvaro sat. His outdoor scent wafted around her. Being pregnant always made her more sensitive and Alvaro smelled of pine forests and sage, a unique outdoors smell that she liked.

"May I be bold enough to speak freely before I open this?" Alvaro said, holding the scroll on his lap, his thumb poised to break the seal.

"Of course," she said.

He cleared his throat. "No matter what is contained in here, I want you to know that I am so humbled to know you."

She tipped her head and studied his dark eyes.

"You have faced trials and tribulations as a woman, as an empress, but you forge your own path."

"I am not sure what you mean."

"Your Majesty, I bear witness to your wise council, and your ability to see an entire picture before it is painted in reality. It makes me proud to know you, to be within your circle. For many women would not step beyond the boundaries their gender dictates."

"You believe I step beyond my boundaries?" She raised her eyebrows.

"As an empress should." He bowed his head.

"I thank you for the kind compliment." She studied his face; his cheeks had reddened slightly. "But please read. Let us find out of the archduchess and the King of France's mother have also stepped from their paths as women."

Alvaro uncurled the scroll and held it up.

She sat back, gripping the chair and staring at the empty fire grate.

"'Esteemed friend, Isabella of Portugal, Queen of Spain, Holy Roman Empress.'" Alvaro paused. "'I write to you with news that I hope will be greatly comforting after our last communications.'"

"The letter I sent her," Isabella interrupted. "About the planned duel."

Alvaro nodded and continued to read. "'I will start at the beginning and tell you that Louise de Savoy and I were both pleased to hear from you. We made contact and the king's mother added into her communication to me that while we must necessarily contend and argue, she sincerely hoped that we would be able to meet without anger or ill will.'"

"That is a good sign." Isabella nodded.

"'So we planned to meet on the border, at Cambria,'" Alvaro went on. "'We were both aware we had many eyes upon us. But despite little confidence in our success—for ambassadors and ministers alike believed we would achieve nothing because of the enmity of France and Spain—I hope we proved them wrong.'"

"Me too."

"'My dear Isabella,'" Alvaro continued. "'I will confess I took with me twenty-four archers, for I know what a snake her son can be. I had to presume such a trait of his mother too. She had told me she would bring only her ladies and nobility, a ban on weapons, for what if we had threatened a duel like the very one we wished to offset?'"

Isabella chuckled. "Wise move."

"'And Louise de Savoy was true to her word. Arriving only with her daughter, her chaplain, her painter, and a handful of choristers.'"

"Quite the selection."

"Indeed." Alvaro revealed some more of the scroll's beautiful, swirling handwriting. "She goes on, listen. 'We sat for some three weeks negotiating. I played my hands cleverly and kept my ear to the ground concerning other developments. At every moment, I fought for the emperor, my beloved nephew and your gracious husband, hoping to make the treaty work in his favor.'"

"This is sounding promising."

"'I have to inform you that Louise is a formidable woman, greatly intelligent, superbly educated, and quite honestly as good an opponent, if not better, than any man.'"

"Oh." Isabella sagged. "Perhaps it did not go well and the duel is still set."

"Let us read on." Alvaro paused. "'We negotiated for three weeks, all day, every day. Sometimes indoors, sometimes in the courtyard. It was a hard task and I feared suddenly being taken hostage by Francis at any moment as repayment to Charles for holding him and his sons prisoner.'"

"That would have been awful." Isabella shook her head and pressed her hand to her chest.

"'Eventually,'" Alvaro read, "'we came to an agreement and signed a treaty on behalf of both Francis, King of France, and Charles, Holy Roman Emperor, which effectively rids the need of the duel to which Charles challenged Francis.'"

"Oh, thank the dear Lord." Isabella raised her eyes heavenward. "She did it. What a godsend." Her eyes stung with relief and a knot between her shoulder blades eased a fraction. "Does she say what she secured?"

"Yes, the archduchess agreed to release the king's sons for a considerable ransom...two million écu." He blew out a breath and shook his head. "That is a lot of money."

"It is indeed."

"She then goes on to say... 'The ransom will be paid in cash, which will agree with Charles very much. Another term is that Eleanor of Austria will indeed marry Francis, a situation which has lingered too long without happening despite her journeying there in preparation a long time ago.'" He hesitated, then read, "'Also, under the terms of this peace treaty, Francis has renounced his claims to Italian lands, Artois, and Flanders, though he has retained Burgundy.'"

"Charles has given up on Burgundy despite it being his grandmother's title." Isabella frowned as she thought. "So that will not distress him. And Margaret is right—that is a handsome ransom and will go toward paying off the high price of the Italian wars."

"The emperor will be pleased, don't you agree?" Alvaro said.

"Yes. Yes I do." She stood, suddenly feeling light after weeks of being weighed down. She'd been unable to sleep because of images of Charles dying on a French field, Francis standing over him wielding a weapon and wearing an ugly, victorious expression.

"You did the right thing," Alvaro said. "Asking for help in giving both men an honorable retreat from the duel."

"It was my worst vision, that duel." She shook her head. "No, there are probably more frightening thoughts, but that one seemed so close and Charles so set on it."

"I agree." He stood. "Your Majesty, I…"

"Yes?" She tipped her head and studied him. For some reason, he looked a little apprehensive. A little coy.

He removed his hat and pressed it against his chest. "I want you to know that I am your most devoted servant." He paused. Swallowed. "I could never aid another lady of nobility. I am yours, at your total and utter disposal. Whatever you need. You only have to ask and I shall give it. Anything."

"I thank you, Alvaro." She touched his hand. "You are a great comfort when Charles is away."

He blinked and looked up at her, his lips trembling a little. "My heart beats for you, Empress," he whispered. "What I am trying to say is I will never want to be at another woman's side. My heart *only* beats for you."

"Oh…I see." And she did. The love and adoration he had for her was pouring from his eyes. "And I also see that my husband was wise indeed to leave you here, with me. As my companion and protector."

He nodded and opened his mouth to speak.

She quickly intercepted whatever it was he was about to say, fearing it could not be unsaid. "When I say my prayers this night I will send thanks to God that you are at my side, as my devoted servant and aide."

He replaced his hat, swallowed tightly, his Adam's apple bobbing, then turned. "My life is dedicated to you." He stepped away.

"Alvaro," she called.

"Yes?" He turned, his breath hitching.

"Could you organize a meeting with the Cortes so I can relay the information you have just brought me?"

"Of course, Your Majesty." He bowed, his eyes on the ground. "I'll do it at once."

⇶⫸⫷⇷

"DONA! DONA! IT is time." Isabella stiffened, gripping her belly. She was in the courtyard embroidering in the pleasant November sunlight. "Oh!"

She closed her eyes, bright lights flashing behind her lids as the wave of pain spreading over her abdomen increased. This was her third labor, but still the shock of the intense pain took her by surprise, almost as though she'd forgotten how painful the others had been.

"Your Majesty." Dona was at her side, holding her hand. "Your Majesty, I am here."

Isabella gritted her teeth and waited for the agony to slide away and give her breath back.

Which it did after several biting moments.

She opened her eyes. "I felt it a little overnight, but it came to nothing, and now…now it is here with full force."

Dona pressed her hand to Isabella's forehead. "Let us get you inside."

"Yes. I will try." She fought to find the power in her legs to stand, but already, they were weak, as though her body were only concentrating on expelling the child in her swollen belly.

"Let me help." Alvaro was suddenly at her side, one strong arm around her and the other there for her to grip on to.

"I thank you."

"We must hurry," Dona said. "Her waters have gone."

It was then Isabella was aware of the wetness between her legs. She groaned in embarrassment, but the sound quickly switched to a gasp of pain as another contraction besieged her.

"What is happening?" Luisa's voice. "Oh...I see. I will fetch the midwife at once."

"And order hot water. Ensure we have everything we need."

"Naturally, I will see to all of that," Luisa snapped and she was then gone.

Alvaro helped Isabella from the courtyard and into the corridor that led to her bedchamber. She clung to him, glad of his strength and calm, but she wished it were Charles with her. Her husband. The father of the child trying to push from her body.

Soon she was in her bedchamber being helped to lie down. Another contraction gripped her and she clasped her belly and held her breath, waiting for the pain to go.

"You should leave now, Alvaro," Dona said. "We women will tend her."

"But—?"

"Go!" Luisa's voice. "This is women's work."

She sensed Luisa and Dona fussing with her. Then another set of hands, the midwife, feeling between her legs.

"He is coming fast," the midwife said. "In a rush to get into this world."

Isabella flopped her head back onto the pillow knowing she would only get a moment of respite before the next tight agony wrapped around her torso.

"Where is the warmed olive oil?" the midwife demanded.

"Here." Dona's voice though it sounded distant.

A cool flannel was set on Isabella's head. Luisa stroked her hair. "The pain will be over soon."

"It is God's will." Isabella gasped. "For Eve's sins." She groaned and fisted the sheet.

"Shh...soon, you will hold your babe."

Her legs were parted, warm oil applied. "This will stop you tearing," the midwife said. "For this is going to be a gallop into the world and—"

Isabella cried out, the pain and the urge to push all-consuming. It was out of her control and she bore down, working with her body now.

"I see the head," Dona said.

"Argh!" Isabella screamed. This child was bursting from her, stretching her to the point she could not bear it.

And then there was a strange kind of relief.

"The head is out." The midwife set her hand on Isabella's stomach. "You are doing so well. One more gentle push. Don't force it."

"It's out... It's..." She was once again gripped by pain and this time, it was accompanied by a slithering, then a falling, as though something had dropped from her.

"You did it," Luisa said excitedly. "Your babe is born."

"And so quickly," Dona said. "We hardly had time to get you on the bed."

Isabella was breathing fast, the pain slipping to the shadows of her memory. "Is it a son?" She was struggling to see the child. The midwife had cut the cord and scooped the tiny babe up in a blanket. She was rubbing its back.

"Why isn't the baby crying?" Luisa asked with a wobble in her voice.

"The child will live," the midwife said determinedly as she rubbed with more vigor.

And then a high-pitched wail rang around the bedchamber.

"Oh, thanks be to God," Isabella said, holding out her arms. "Give...to me..."

"Here." The midwife laid the child in her arms. "You did well, Your Majesty."

"Thank you." She moved the blanket and looked at her child's tiny penis. "A son. The emperor has another son." Her heart filled. "He will be pleased."

"As are we all." Luisa kissed Isabella's head tenderly. "You have great strength, and great fertility, Your Majesty."

Isabella smiled. Happiness filled her heart. She couldn't wait to write to Charles and tell him the good news. Perhaps it would hasten his return to Spain and into her arms.

CHAPTER FOURTEEN

Bologna
Italy

"MUST I DEAL with every danger?" Charles muttered as he paced toward Bologna's cathedral. "Suleiman marching on Vienna, Florence under siege, and now Luther's heretic poison spreading down from Germany."

"As emperor, you are one of the twin pillars of the Church, together with the pope." Bishop Gabriel walked quickly at his side, his scarlet robe fluttering around his ankles. He was a young man with a keen mind and sharp wit.

Charles had become accustomed to his company and council of late. And as usual, Gabriel was right in what he said. It was Charles's duty to dampen the fire Luther's thesis had created. "The divisions sparked by Luther have dragged my empire into a religious battle I did not want."

"None of us wanted it," Gabriel said. "It is a black mark on Christendom."

"I am not above some reform," Charles went on. "There is a need for the removal of abuses of many types, our own black marks, but this…this is an open and raw wound that will not heal and is in fact worsening as time goes by." He paused and looked up at the cathedral's impressive portico. It was early morning, the sun only just rising and casting an ochre glow on the pillars and brickwork. There were few people around, which meant Charles could take his morning prayer in peace.

Not that he felt peaceful on this morn.

"I am sure God will give you the answer," Gabriel said calmly.

"Mm." Charles entered the cool shadows of the church. As he walked toward the altar, he admired the frescos once again and thought how Isabella would enjoy them.

Isabella. If only she were with him. He was sure he would find a solution to all of his imperial problems if he could hammer out each with her. Their two minds together were much better than one, more than double, for they were so in tune.

His heart squeezed. He missed her. His arms ached at night when he lay in his bed. And still each morning he rolled over, reaching for her, wishing to find her warm, soft body to hold as the birds started their song.

He took a pew, a commoners' pew, and dipped his head.

Gabriel, respectfully, sat just behind him and to the right.

"Heavenly Father," Charles whispered, holding his rosary. "Please give me strength and wisdom." He went quiet, preferring to have his conversation with God in private.

After several minutes, he opened his eyes and stared at an image of Christ on the cross. "I am going to have to make every effort to unify the Church," he said. "And the first thing I will do is convene a meeting of church council, including the pope, to address these evils that have arisen."

"I hope you are successful."

"You don't sound optimistic." He turned and looked at Gabriel.

Gabriel sighed. "I know they think this is a German problem only."

"It is a problem for all of God's good people."

"I agree." Gabriel nodded and pressed his lips together.

"You appear to have more to say." Charles raised his eyebrows.

"I do not wish to speak out of turn."

"I command you to speak. I trust your judgment."

"I thank you, Your Majesty." Gabriel dipped his head. "I believe it would be wise to do what you can, rather than what you wish to be able to do at this stage."

Charles frowned, sighed, then turned back to the image of Christ. "If Francis hadn't been such a ludicrous and ineffectual king…if he'd taken this protestant problem in hand when I asked, we would not be where we are now."

"That is in the past, a past we cannot change."

Charles let the words settle. Again, Gabriel was right. He also blamed himself somewhat for spending so much time in Spain and also not keeping a dampener on the protestant fire. "So with that in mind," he said, thinking as he spoke, "and if our wish is not to let these ideas spread from Germany to the Low Countries, I must have council also with my brother, Ferdinand, at the earliest opportunity. He is in Vienna, a strategic place for action."

"A wise move," Gabriel said. "Though may I advise one other thing?"

"Naturally." Charles stood and waved his hand in the air. "Tell me."

Gabriel also rose. "Hold your moves close. The waters are volatile and there is much to lose."

"I agree. I need to take a strong line because the risk to our faith is enormous. I must tread as gently as a kitten though be ready to bite like a lion."

A sudden rush of air blustered into the calm space followed by the interruption of banging footfalls.

Charles reached for the dagger he kept in his belt, gripping the hilt. "Who goes there?"

"Your Majesty." A breathless voice. "Your Majesty, an envoy has just delivered this."

A courtier, dressed in red, cloak flapping, rushed down the altar.

"Give it to me." Charles strode up to him, hand outstretched.

He snatched the scroll from the puffing, young man, who immediately bent over double, dragging in breaths.

"It is from the empress," Charles said, tearing at the seal.

His heart skipped and his stomach roiled. If she'd sealed it personally, then she must have fared well through childbirth. Though there was still news of his child to hear.

His hands were shaking as he uncurled it and his stomach clenched. What would lie within?

Barely able to focus, he read the first few words written in her delicate, looping handwriting.

Most beloved and esteemed husband,

I write to inform you of the birth of our son, Ferdinand. He arrived quickly into the world after the first cold night of winter. He is small but loud and already, Philip and little Maria are quite taken with their brother.

I send my prayers daily that you will soon be returned to us.

Godspeed, my love.

Your devoted wife, Isabella.

"A son!" He grinned at the courtier. "I have another son!"

"Congratulations." Gabriel clasped his hands in prayer. "What a joyous blessing for the empire."

"It is, indeed!" Charles dragged Gabriel into a hug.

Gabriel gasped, evidently a little shocked by the intimate gesture, but then slapped his back. "We have great thanks to give."

"We do indeed." He released Gabriel and threw up his arms. "We will feast and drink wine. I will think no more of imperial problems, for today at least." His heart was thumping wildly and he had the urge to dance and sing and run up and down the church aisle.

But of course he didn't. He was emperor, after all. It was only Isabella who would have witnessed him lose control that way.

And she wasn't here.

Which pained him afresh. If only she were, if only they had not had to be parted. But he simply couldn't move his entire family with him when he went away on business. It wasn't practical, not least when she was with child.

"My wife is proving an able regent, but I must go to her soon," he said. "At the soonest opportunity." He flicked his hand through the air. "With the Ladies' Peace in Cambrai now signed, God bless the Archduchess Margaret of Austria, the French wars have finally concluded."

"And don't forget, you must be crowned by Pope Clement," Gabriel said. "And if I may say so, you can now afford to do it with considerable style."

"Exactly!" He turned to the statue of Christ, bowed low, then turned and walked from the cathedral into the cool, morning air. "It is all the more important I am crowned now that I have another heir to the Holy Roman Empire. Ferdinand. Prince Ferdinand, a fine name for a fine boy."

><>><><<<

CHARLES WOKE IN *Palazzo Comunale* to the sound of distant bells. It was his thirtieth birthday and the day of his coronation.

Finally.

It had taken many negotiations with Pope Clement to reach this point. They'd had to settle the outstanding areas of contention in Italy, which had been no easy task—the pontiff had refused to crown him until this point had been resolved.

Fortunately, their talks had been punctuated with splendid festivities, tournaments, horse races, and bull baiting, all of which were public so Charles could show off his prowess and skills.

Because Charles intended to make the most of his traveling to boost his reputation. He'd ordered wood carvings, pamphlets, and medallions to commemorate his visit to Italy and had now become used to the cries of *"Carlo, Carlo, Impero, Impero, Cesare, Cesare"* when he traveled through the city. Something he wouldn't have gotten in Rome, as his reputation there was still raw after the bad behavior of his army.

He walked to the window and looked out at the piazza. Triumphal arches full of imperial images—victories, generals, Roman emperors—lined the streets. Already, people were loitering, waiting to see him, to shower him in adoration and coins, fruit, and candies.

He turned when there was a knock at the door. "Enter."

Mercurino de Gattinara, Charles's chancellor, stepped in. Tall, stiff-faced and pale he was already dressed in his finery. "I bid you a good morning."

"And you, my friend. You look very becoming in your gold cloth."

"I thank you." He bowed his head. "Emperor."

"It is quite the jostle out there already."

"The people are excited to see you. It is a day that will go down in history."

"As it should." He lifted the lid from a plate and smeared honey on bread. "Antonio is happy with the preparations?"

"Yes, you are to leave from an open window from this building. From it you will take a newly constructed raised, wooden walkway to the top of the steps at the front of the basilica of San Petrino. That way, you will not be touched by the people, but be seen by many from down below."

Charles nodded and poured milk.

"There is a problem?" Mercurino asked.

"No, not at all, it's…"

"What is missing? Please tell me so I can make it right."

"I am afraid even if I tell you that will not be possible."

"I can try."

"I wish," he said, "that my wife were here. She is empress—she deserves to be part of the ceremony."

"Do you wish us to delay it so she can journey here?"

"No. That is not what I mean." He paused. "I just *wish* she were here." He pressed his hand to his chest. "She is a part of me, if that makes sense."

"I am happy that you have such love in your life."

"I am indeed blessed. But no, we cannot delay. I have promised my brother, Ferdinand, a visit. These pesky problems in Germany do not go away."

"The good people of Italy have every faith that you will find a solution."

Shortly after the clock had struck eight A.M., Charles's procession climbed through a second story window and set off on the new planked walkway.

Ahead of him were cupbearers, pages, stewards, chamberlains, military officers, councilors, ministers, and envoys from across Europe. He held his chin high as his plain, black robe swished around him. He was devoid of finery, a symbol of purity arriving before God.

He passed tapestries of golden cloth, and a great ball with an eagle on top swung from a tall building, showering his procession in scent.

Just as they'd reached the entrance to the Basilica, there was a crash and a commotion behind him. He turned. "What is that?"

"A collapse, I believe," the Duke of Savoy said anxiously. He placed his hand protectively over the crown he carried.

"We should help," Charles said, taking a step back.

"No, Your Majesty," the Marquis of Montferrato said, gripping the orb. "I urge you to keep going. The soldiers will attend."

Charles fought his instinct to offer assistance as he heard shouts and another crash. Instead, he allowed himself to be bustled past a row of soldiers with pikes into the cool of the Basilica.

Suddenly, calm surrounded him. He took a deep breath and imagined Isabella at his side.

"You couldn't help back there, my love. You would have caused more harm as people rushed to see you, to touch you, to be blessed by you."

He knew that was what she would say and she'd be right in doing so.

He closed his eyes and pictured her pretty face. Her delicate nose, smiling mouth, and eyes that looked at him as though she could see right into his soul.

A lone trumpet sounded and he followed his procession down the aisle.

Pope Clement, wearing his traditional papal triple tiara, awaited him. He was flanked by purple-robed cardinals and old archbishops who looked on sternly.

For a moment, Charles had a rush of nerves, his stomach flipped, but then he heard Isabella's voice again.

"This is your destiny. This is what God wants for you."

He kept on walking and finally drew up beside the pontiff.

The ceremony began. He was invested with a heavy cloak that dragged on his shoulders despite his broad strength. The crown of Lombardy was placed upon his head and pressed down to keep it as secure as possible. He was given the orb and scepter and then mass was celebrated.

When it was over cannons on the city walls boomed, trumpets and drums played in the piazzas, and he and Pope Clement walked hand in hand down the center of the basilica. Charles felt like he were floating, as though he were somewhere between heaven and Earth. He'd achieved his ultimate goal, to create unity between the Church and his empire. Power was now his without question. What could stop him from achieving all of his religious, political, and imperial aims? Nothing. Nothing could stop him.

Or at least that was what it felt like on this splendid day.

CHAPTER FIFTEEN

ISABELLA LIFTED THE hem of her dress and ran from the dark room. A scream grew in the depths of her chest as she took the stairs. Her heart bled, her skin burned, and her stomach threatened to bring up her breakfast.

"Isabella!" Dona called after her.

She kept on running, agony infusing her blood. She wanted what had just happened to be reframed. To be undone. To be taken back.

Her poor baby.

"Please, wait…" Dona's footfalls. "I beg you."

But it was as though the devil himself were carrying her and she gained speed, rushing down a corridor, then taking a doorway out onto the rooftop terrace.

Still, the scream grew. A feral pain that was a fist inside of her. It would never go. She'd never be rid of it.

The sun beat down on her face, but she didn't feel its heat. The air was filled with the soft sent of flowers, but she didn't notice. She ran to the rampart wall and leaned over it.

At that point, her scream could no longer be contained. It poured from her. Guttural torment. A misery that now lived with in her. No amount of screaming could get the suffering of grief from her system, but on and on she screamed. Eyes screwed up tightly, fingernails clawing the stone work. Tears pouring down her cheeks.

"Your Majesty, please." Dona's voice. "Please, I beg you, come inside." She wrapped her arms around Isabella, but Isabella shook her off.

The screaming continued, tearing at her throat. Deafening her. Never again would she nurse her baby, Ferdinand. He'd been taken to heaven before his time. His innocent little body lifeless at dawn.

"Empress...please...I beg you." Dona was crying too. Isabella could hear it, but she didn't care. She didn't care about anything at that moment other than trying to rid her soul of the python of distress that coiled around her.

Eventually, she became breathless. Tears dripped from her chin and her body shook. She slumped to the floor, curling into a ball and shaking.

"Your Majesty." Dona dropped next to her and stroked her hair. "What can I do to help?"

There was nothing anyone could do to help. She must bear this alone.

Charles. She needed Charles more than she'd ever needed him.

"Oh, please...please..." Dona said. "You mustn't distress yourself so."

If Isabella had had the energy, she'd have admonished Dona. As if she had any control over her distress. It was alive within her. A palpable, evil being.

More footfalls. "I just heard." Alvaro's voice. "Oh, Your Majesty..."

He was next to her too, his hand on her back. "I am so sorry. So very sorry that you must bear this pain. This awful pain in your soul."

She sniffed and dashed at tears, tried and failed to hold in a gulping sob.

"Your little boy is with God now," he went on, rubbing a circle on her shoulder. "He is at peace with Our Father."

Silent tears fell now, dampening her cheeks. She was locked in her dark, torturous world. A curled up ball of pain. If she never moved again, that would suit her. If she died and went to her son, that would also suit her.

"Come, Your Majesty, let us get you to your bedchamber," Dona said, trying to dab Isabella's cheeks with a kerchief. "Your grief should be a private affair."

"I do not care…" Isabella wailed. "Who sees my grief." She raised her head. "The whole of Spain will mourn with me. The loss of their little prince is a tragedy of national import."

"Yes, yes, it is." Dona nodded, her eyes red-rimmed.

"We will make the death announcement," Alvaro said. "An official three days of mourning will follow."

"It is the least he deserves." Isabella sat onto her knees and hugged herself tightly. If she didn't, she was in danger of falling apart.

"He deserved the world," Alvaro said. "And everything in it."

"And now it will never be his." She looked at Alvaro's kind face. He was clearly distraught and much paler than usual. "How can I bear this without Charles at my side?"

"Let me help you," he said softly and he held out his hand. "Let us, your closest and most loyal friends, help you, Your Majesty."

"Friends," she repeated. Her mind was fogged with grief, as though thoughts about anything other than her loss couldn't quite form. "I have lost him, my baby."

"I know." Alvaro nodded and his mouth downturned. "I know. Now come, let us get inside." He took her hand then helped her, along with Dona, to stand.

She allowed it. Her knees were weak and she was suddenly exhausted. The thought of bed appealed, to be in darkness, to cry until she could cry no more and unconsciousness stole her away.

Perhaps she would wake and it would all be a bad dream. Maybe Charles would be sitting on the end of her bed when a new dawn arrived.

They led her indoors. She stared down at her dusty, creased gown, her vision blurred and her eyes stinging.

The cool darkness of her bedchamber was a relief for a split second, then the agony came back over her in a huge wave. Her arms ached to hold her child. Her breasts ached to feed him.

"Come. Come." Dona helped her lie down then gently covered her in a blanket.

Alvaro removed his hat then sat on the bed and took her hand in his. A bold move for a man who was not her husband, but she had other things to worry about.

"What can I do to help?" he asked.

"There is nothing?" Dona said. "Nothing we can do."

"Dona," Alvaro said. "Get Her Majesty some wine, fortified, a good strong one from Jerez."

"Yes, good idea." Dona quickly rushed to the door and called instructions to a servant.

Isabella stared straight ahead at the unlit fire. Tears still rolled down her cheeks, but she'd given up swiping them away.

"I will prepare a statement and have it pinned to the gates of the palace," Alvaro said gently. "With your permission."

"Yes. You have it." She nodded.

"And send message to the bishop that a funeral must be planned."

A sob choked her.

"Oh, Your Majesty, my beautiful empress, I am so sorry. So very sorry."

She gulped. "I need you to do one more thing, Alvaro."

"Anything. Anything on God's good Earth that I can do or give to you, I will. You know that is my promise to you."

"Yes, Alvaro, I know." She squeezed his warm hand. "I need you to write to Charles for me." She paused as her heart squeezed. "He needs to know he has lost the son he never met."

Alvaro lowered his head, his eyes closed. "I will write him, though every word, every letter, will pain me."

"I thank you for taking on the burden, one that I could not bear at this time."

"I will carry whatever weight I can for you." He kissed the large, ruby ring on her finger. "Most beloved empress."

>>><<<

THE YEARS PASSED by. Isabella bottled up her grief as though it were a scream trapped in a jar. Always present but hidden from the outside world. She had two other beautiful children to whom to tend and to educate. Her heart swelled with love at their joy when they discovered simple pleasures in the palace gardens. Philip and Maria were a balm to her grief.

Charles's aunt, the archduchess, had passed on soon after little Ferdinand. Isabella was busy with council and court. Being at the helm meant many decisions had to be made. Seasons came and went, as did Christmas and Easter celebrations, which the children enjoyed, though she always felt hollow—there were too many loved ones missing.

Her nights were long and lonely. Cold, too, during the dark winter months.

And despite her writing to Charles often, his replies were sporadic and infrequent—something which irritated Isabella more than it should have and she was repentant about this often at confession.

She thought of his most recent letter. After reading it one hundred times, the words were etched in her brain.

Most beloved wife, Isabella,

I pick up this quill with a heavy heart that misses you so. If I could mount the fastest steed in the stables and gallop to you, I would this day. But the Turkish menace has increased so much that I have even considered coming to an agreement with the Lutherans in order to prevent worse disaster.

Suleiman and his troops have once again marched east from Is-

tanbul. *I am planning a great expedition against the sultan to fulfill my role as Holy Roman Emperor and Master of the Order of the Golden Fleece. I have honor to uphold as leader of Christendom and I have decided that if the Turk comes in person, which he can only do at the head of a great force, I will go forth with all the forces I can find to resist him.*

I am planning on assembling an army headed by my best commanders at Regensburg, with troops summoned from Germany, the Low Countries, and Italy, then I will navigate down the Danube to meet the enemy head on.

Please pray for me, and the brave Christian soldiers who fight for our reputation and our God, my love. When this is over I will be at your side again. You will be in my arms again. And we will love and laugh and be at peace the way we were in Granada all of those years ago.

May God protect you and our children on Earth and in heaven.

My emperor's heart, body, and soul is yours.

Charles

When would Charles return to Spain?

Impatience clawed at her. Irritation needled her. Frustration itched.

There had been word from other sources that there had been a great gun battle at Koszeg before her husband had even gotten that far west. It had damaged the sultan's army so much, he'd retreated, his show of aggression and parade of strength not achieving anything for him.

Surely, after all of this time, Charles would see he was needed here. There was nothing for him to do in Vienna now.

"Your Majesty, have you made a decision?"

"I beg your pardon?" She looked up at the five councilors who sat around the long, polished table.

"About raising taxes to fund defenses in Granada."

She brought her mind back to the matter at hand. "It depends how real we think the Ottoman threat from the sea is." She looked at Alvaro. "Have we had further news?"

"There have been no reported sightings of Turkish galleys in the area, but we must remember they can build them quickly and sail as fast as the wind."

"The stories of Turkish plundering around the Mediterranean have spread throughout my kingdom." She tapped her fingers on the table. "I believe the people will be willing to fund these defenses to stop it from happening here. Or at least, hope that we can stop it from happening here." What would Charles have done? That was a question she often asked herself. But she had to answer the question herself because Charles had left her as regent. She had the final say on all such matters.

"Your Majesty?" Alvaro pressed.

A knot had formed in her right shoulder, a darting pain that made her wince as she tried to get it more comfortable.

"What is it?" Alvaro asked worriedly.

"A pain. Tension, I presume." She cupped her hand over her left shoulder and rubbed.

"Allow me?" Alvaro reached toward her, closing the gap between them.

"No!" she snapped. She held his eye contact until he looked away. "That will not be necessary." Alvaro had to be careful. He could be too familiar at times. The last thing she needed was gossip.

A silence extended. And then some more.

"Your Majesty, the taxes," one of the councilors said eventually.

The expectant expressions around the table helped her concentrate. After a moment, she nodded. "Yes, let us raise the tax. We will also print pamphlets explaining why we need to do this. I will sign it myself as the people's queen and empress. This will show them of my promise and my duty to protect our lands." She balled her fists. "We will not be at the mercy of the Turks."

"Very good, Your Majesty," Alvaro said. "Your people are lucky to have you."

"I thank you." She stood and brushed the creases from the front of her gown. Glancing out of the window, she saw a figure riding into the courtyard. Dressed in a black cloak, hood up, he was followed by several knights in full body armor.

Her heart skipped.

Could it be?

Was it?

She rushed to the window, pressed her palms onto it, and stared out, unblinking.

The figure drew to a halt on the cobblestones. The horse threw up its head and whinnied, its lustrous, raven mane shimmering in the sunlight.

"Charles?" she whispered.

Alvaro was at her side, gripping the windowsill. "Is it he?"

She didn't need to answer because the figure dropped his hood and looked directly up at her.

Her heart stuttered. Her breath caught.

Finally.

"Oh, thank the Lord." She kissed the cross that sat around her neck. "The emperor has returned to us."

The councilors rushed to the window in a scrape of chair legs and banging footfalls.

Isabella felt as though she'd been nailed to the spot. But even though she was perfectly still, a rush of emotions raced through her. Had he not thought to tell her of his intentions to return? She could have prepared herself for him. Been ready in every way.

But then her body took flight. Almost of its own volition. She gathered her gown and rushed from the room. She took the steps much faster than she should, careening past servants setting a table for luncheon, and then ran out into the courtyard.

He was off his horse, his cloak over the arm of a stablehand who now held his horse's reins. He was as tall and broad as ever, though more tanned, likely from days in the saddle. His boots were dusty, as were his black breeches and his brown leather belt held a sheathed sword and a bone-handled dagger.

He spun toward her. His eyes widened and he stepped forward, arms outstretched. "My love!"

The sound of his deep, husked voice had a sob springing from her throat and she threw herself at him.

The embrace that caught her was tight and desperate. He pulled her close, their bodies aligning. A low groan rumbled from his chest as his mouth captured hers. It was a passionate, desperate kiss that reminded her of all the times they'd been together sweating, naked, finding pleasure.

She moaned softly and filled her fingers with his hair, pulling him nearer—all thoughts of the knights, councilors, and courtiers around her evaporating. Finally, with him at her side, she'd be able to breathe, to sleep, to live again.

He broke the kiss and pulled back, holding her face in his palms. "I am so happy to be here." He smiled.

"And I am happy that you're here." She gazed into his eyes. "But why didn't you send word that you were coming?"

"I wanted to arrive incognito. I wanted no fanfare from the city."

"But...but I'm your wife. You should have told me." She frowned and remembered all the times she'd watched the entrance to the palace, wishing for an envoy to arrive with a letter from Charles. "You should have told me so much more than you did. You barely wrote to me and it's been many years."

"I am sorry." He raised his eyebrows. "If that bothered you."

"*Bothered* me!" She pushed at him and stepped away from his embrace. "Yes, it bothered me. Considerably. I am empress, queen, and your wife. You should have written often, the way I did to you." She stabbed her thumb against her chest. "You made me feel forgotten, forgotten by you, my husband."

"Forgotten?" He frowned and shook his head. "How could I forget you, Isabella? You are the love of my life. The mother of my children and—"

"Yes, the mother of your children. Children who barely know you." A vat of bottled-up grief bubbled inside of her. "And when our child died, where were you? You didn't come even then to my side."

"Isabella, please." He held out his palms. "If I could have—"

"You are Holy Roman Emperor—you can do whatever you want." Her voice raised, she waggled her index finger at him. "So do not tell me you could not have come to me. Could not have grieved with me. Do not tell me that because I do not believe it."

"I wept." He touched the cross at his neck. "I wept and I sent prayers to God to look after our little Ferdinand."

"That is not enough." She tipped her chin, battling to hold back tears. "Your distant sorrow and your prayers were not enough." She set her lips in a tight line then spun, once again gathering the hem of her gown. "Nowhere near enough." She stomped back over the courtyard, her vision blurring as her eyes misted.

"Isabella!" Charles called. "Wait."

But she didn't. It wasn't that she wasn't pleased he was home safe after what must have been a long and arduous journey—she was—but that didn't mean she couldn't still be angry with him.

His lack of communication had been hurtful and frustrating. So many times she'd had to make important decisions in his absence. Not that she couldn't make them—it just would have been nice to have had his council the way he so often asked for hers.

"Your Majesty, would you like a—?" a servant asked.

"No." She waved away a bowl of stuffed figs. "Is there cold wine in my chambers?"

"Yes, Your Majesty. Of course, Your Majesty."

"Good." She stamped up the staircase, her anger a blustering frenzy. Charles called her name again, but she kept on going.

She reached her room, burst in, and threw the bolt.

CHAPTER SIXTEEN

I SABELLA LEANED HER back on the door and stared at a curtain wafting in the draft of an open window. She was breathing fast and her heart thudded.

For so long, she'd prayed for this moment, her husband's return, but now that he was here, all she felt was anger. It was hot and viscous within her and she couldn't control it.

The door handle rattled. "Isabella!" Charles shouted through the wood. "Let me in."

"No."

"I beg you."

"You cannot just show up after all of this time without word and expect everything to return to the day you left." She pushed away from the door. Her scalp was suddenly itchy and she dragged at her headdress, tossing it to a chair. It missed and rolled to the floor.

"I am sorry. Please open the door." The handle rattled again.

"*Sorry* is not enough."

"So what is?" His voice was a low growl now. He was getting frustrated.

Good.

"I do not know," she said, slamming her hands onto her hips. "I haven't thought about it."

"So think."

"Leave me be."

"I have traveled hundreds of miles to be with you, through forests and over mountains. I have dodged bandits and pirates and sat in the saddle many a long day and night. So if you don't open the door, I'll—"

"What? Go away again?" She marched up to it. "For another *four years*?" she shouted at the wood.

He was silent for a moment. "I can see that was too long. It will never happen again."

Her jaw clenched so tight, she wondered if bone might crack. And she balled her fists until her fingernails cut into her palms.

"Isabella, let us talk, face to face, my love."

"I don't want to. Not yet."

Again, he was silent, then, "So when?"

"Perhaps later." She walked to the table and picked up a jug of wine. After pouring herself a goblet, she drank deep. "If my anger with you has abated with the passage of time."

"Dearest Isabella, I love you so. Please do not be angered by me."

"I cannot help it. I have felt so alone for so long."

"But I am here now. You are not alone anymore."

"Perhaps I have gotten used to it." She topped up her wine. "Now leave me. Go and speak with Alvaro. He will inform you of the latest council decisions."

"But...may I see the children?"

"No, they are studying. I do not wish for them to be disturbed." She could practically feel his tension vibrating into the room. Was he going to argue, assert his authority, and disturb the children's lessons? Or would he concede to her decision for the sake of not aggravating her further?

"I understand," he said, his voice calm but strained.

She could imagine him standing with arms crossed, feet hip-width apart and chest puffed up. Keeping a tight grasp of his self-control. He wasn't a man used to being told *no*. Not getting what he wanted was unchartered territory for the Holy Roman Emperor. Having others deny him his wishes was no doubt a new experience.

But she wasn't any other person. She was his wife and she had ruled with great success in his absence. And he would just have to get used to the fact that he couldn't order her at his whim.

"I can understand why you are so perturbed by me and I will leave you alone so your agitation can settle."

Agitation settle!

"That would be very wise," she said with a frown. "For an empress whose blood is boiling is a dangerous beast to be around." She finished her wine in a few quick gulps then replaced the goblet in her hand with her Bible.

She stilled, waiting for him to reply.

But he didn't and she heard the murmur of voices. Alvaro was at his side, perhaps? And then footfalls fading down the corridor.

She flopped into a chair and rested her head back. The sudden silence seemed to swim around her, making her ears ring and sending waves of dizziness into her head.

How quickly her day had changed. She'd gone from making plans to raise taxes and order the printing of pamphlets to sitting alone with an emotional ball of energy that was bouncing around inside of her like an excited, yapping puppy.

"After all this time…" she whispered, closing her eyes. "He just rides back into town thinking nothing has changed."

She sighed, a long expulsion of air that she hoped would take her frustration with it.

It wasn't that she *wanted* to be angry with Charles for his long absence, or irritated by his unannounced arrival, but she couldn't help it. They were the feelings that were being thrown at her and she was taking them like slaps to the face and punches to her guts.

She opened her Bible and tried to read, something that always calmed her. But she could barely see the words. They blurred and fused together on the page.

After a few minutes, she closed the velvet-and-gold-bound book and put it aside, reaching for her rosary and playing it through her fingers. She was a patient and prudent woman, she knew that, but Charles could create a passion and fury in her that was off her usual compass.

Luisa had once told Isabella that when she was anxious she thought about relaxing her fingers and toes, and then her arms and legs, then her shoulders and chest and neck. Taking her time. Breathing deep and trying to let her thoughts blow away with each breath.

Isabella tried this now, wriggling then relaxing her toes, flexing and un-flexing her fingers. But after a few minutes, far from being able to rid her mind of thoughts, all that came to her were images of Charles. She remembered the feel of his lips on hers in the courtyard, his urgent embrace, and the heat of his body through his clothing.

She wriggled and her breath hitched. The knot in her shoulder hurt. She was at war with wanting him and not wanting him. A tug between her legs had her remembering the last time they'd lain together, all those years ago.

There was no denying she wanted him still, perhaps more than back then. Her body had been drawn to his the moment she'd seen him through the window. Running like a *loca* woman into his arms. Throwing all sense of decorum to the ground as she'd kissed him with undisguised lust.

"Oh, Charles," she said, standing and abandoning all thoughts of trying to relax. "What you do to me. God only knows my suffering."

There was a sudden knock on the door.

"Who is it?" she snapped.

"It is me, my love. I have brought more wine, and I have something else for you."

"What do you have?" She glanced at the empty wine jug. She'd made short work of it.

"Let me show you. I beg you."

"You *beg*?"

"Yes. I will beg on my knees if that is what you desire."

That wasn't a bad idea. She clamped her lips together, and, irritated by herself, strode to the door. She slid the lock free from the bolt hole but didn't turn the handle, then she marched back to the window and stared out at the city's terracotta roofs and rolling, vine-filled hills beyond.

The door opened, slowly, creaking as it did so.

Instantly, the temperature in the room seemed to change. Her skin prickled and her nipples tightened. Charles was so much more than just a man stepping into her chambers. He was an emperor, a king...her husband and lover.

The door closed. She heard the lock slide into place again.

It was clear he wasn't going to be disturbed now that he'd managed to gain entry.

She watched his reflection walk to the table and refill the jug with wine. He poured two cups full. And then he stared at her, hands on his hips, chin tilted upward.

A tremble attacked her belly. She'd perhaps forgotten how big and broad he was, how strength oozed from him. Far from looking battle weary, her husband appeared to have thrived during his adventures.

"I should have sent word," he said, "of my intention to arrive back in Valladolid. Please forgive me for giving you such a wretched surprise."

"It was not wretched." She turned, arms folded across her chest. "I am glad that you are alive to make the journey, to come back to me. It is what I have prayed for every day."

"So if you are glad"—his mouth downturned and he shrugged— "why do you look like you would set the archers upon me, given the chance?"

"Do you really not understand?"

He picked up a goblet, drank, then set it aside. "I am trying to understand."

"So let me be clearer." She sucked in a breath. "You left here four years ago, and you have barely written to me. I have heard of much of your news through Alvaro's communications with your traveling companions and aides."

"Again, I am sorry. But in my defense, I have been busy."

"Not so busy that you should ignore your wife." She pointed at him. "Allow your wife to spend many months wondering about your heart...your devotion."

"I am utterly devoted to you." He took a step closer but stopped when she frowned deeper. "You are my one and only love. I swear. I have lived like a priest since I last saw you. I am a celibate man."

She studied him through narrowed eyes. "You swear?"

"On the Bible." He reached for it and spread his palm over the top of it. "I swear I have never known another woman since the day we married. I love you, Isabella."

Her heart melted slightly at the words, but she didn't repeat them.

"Please, accept my apology," he said. "I would never have been so remiss had I known it would hurt you so."

"Yes, that is what it did. It hurt me, deeply."

"And upon hearing that, I wish to flay myself for giving you one second of pain."

"That will not be necessary." She folded her arms again. Her body had come to life, just by being in the same room as him. Her blood flowed hotter, a tug between her legs quivered, and the rest of the room, the palace, had faded from her attention. "But what *will* be necessary," she said, tilting her chin, "is for you to beg for my forgiveness."

"'Beg'?"

"You said you would." She nodded at the door. "And I would like to see it."

He swallowed noisily and frowned. "I beg your forgiveness."

"Oh, no. Not like that." She nodded at the red rug she was standing on. "Beg on your knees, the way you said you would."

His jaw tensed—it was coated in stubble—and his eyes narrowed. "I am emperor. People kneel before me."

"I am not *people*. I am your wife."

He was quiet.

"And you have wronged me."

Again, he said nothing.

"Are you not good for your word, Charles?"

"You know I am." His voice had deepened to almost a growl. And his face had darkened. But he stepped forward and then dipped to one knee before her, his sword at an angle, the point tapping the rug behind.

"So tell me," she said, pouting and looking at a patch of dust on his tunic's shoulder. "For what, exactly, are you begging my forgiveness?"

"For not writing," he said. "As often as I should have."

"I will forgive that if you promise it will never happen again. I wish for monthly letters when you are absent."

"That is acceptable."

"That is the least you can do."

His jaw tensed.

"What else?"

"And for…" He paused. "And for not informing you of my return."

"I wish to know in future so I can organize a celebratory feast and have the children prepared to see their father. That is not too much to ask, is it?"

"No, it isn't. I will always see that you are informed."

"Good."

He shifted on his knee.

"And…?"

"My love." He took her hand and stared into her face. "I am so sorry I didn't come to you when our baby son died. I should have. I see that now."

Her eyes prickled instantly at the mention of her loss. "You should have. I needed you."

He kissed her knuckles then pressed her hand to his cheek and closed his eyes. "I never even met him."

"I know." A sob choked her and suddenly, she was on her knees, before him. "I wanted you to. I so wanted him to know you. His father, the emperor. It broke my heart that he didn't."

"Isabella." He released her hand and caught her within the circle of his arms. He pulled her close, tucking her head beneath his chin.

She cried and clung to him. The pain that had been secreted away burst out in wretched, gut-wrenching sobs.

He was crying too. She could feel it and hear it. His embrace was desperate and needy.

For the first time in so long, she had the sense that someone understood her pain. Ferdinand had been Charles's child as much as hers.

"My love," he said eventually when her sobs were spent. "Look at me." He captured her face from where they were sitting in a heap on the rug. "Look at me and hear this."

She swallowed, her saliva thick and her cheeks wet. "I am listening."

"A wise priest, Gabriel, he spoke to me when I was lost in my grief." He paused.

"What did he say to you?" she asked softly. "Please, tell me."

"He told me that although our child's life was short and he knew not much of the world, he did know love. Your love. His mother's love. And for that, we must be grateful, for is there a greater thing on God's Earth than the love of a mother? Ferdinand had that. We must let that be a comfort." He kissed her brow. "And I am both humbled and grateful that my son knew you, that you are his mother, the most tender, caring, sweet mother he could wish for."

"Oh, Charles." She touched his cheek. "Those are wise words

indeed." She shook her head. "And I will pray for Gabriel to bring comfort to others in his flock with his wisdom."

"You will get to meet him," Charles said. "For I have found his company most pleasing and he has traveled here with me."

"I would like that. To meet him."

"Good, for I do not wish to apologize any more to my wife, at least not today."

"I do not wish for that, either."

CHAPTER SEVENTEEN

ISABELLA TWISTED HER leg to a more comfortable position, but it didn't help.

"Here, let us get off the floor," Charles said.

He helped her to standing and she brushed out the dust and folds from her gown. She then sat and clasped her hands in her lap.

"Wine?" he asked, offering her a goblet.

"I thank you." She took it.

He removed his sword and set it against the wall. Next came his belt and dagger. He tugged at his tunic, opening the top few buttons. "I forget how hot it is in Spain."

"It is cooling now. Winter is nearly here."

"It is still warm compared to other parts of my empire, where there is snow already falling."

"I should like to see snow one day."

"Then you will...but..." His eyes sparkled and he delved into the pocket of his breeches.

"But what?" She managed a small smile.

"But until then, you shall have this to think of snow." He produced a golden brooch. It was as long as her index finger and shaped like a flower, but not one she recognized. The bloom was like a white church bell hanging down, the clappers protruding from the base.

"It is a snowdrop," Charles said. "A flower that blooms even when the earth is covered in white frost and snow."

"It flowers through snow?"

"Yes, it is small and delicate, but so very strong and hardy." He carefully unclipped it then slid his fingers into her neckline so he could pin it in place without risk of pricking her skin.

She hitched in a breath at his nearness, his masculine, outdoor scent besieging her. His touch had sparks of desire tickling over her breasts and spreading lower.

She stared at his face, at the stubble over his full top lip, and the expression of concentration.

"There," he said, admiring the brooch and pulling back. "It is now with its rightful owner, the empress."

"I thank you. I love it." She rested her fingertips on the gold.

"If I could have brought snow back, I would have." He chuckled and reached for his wine.

"But it would melt."

"Yes, very quickly."

"I remember," he said, looking at a portrait on the wall, "my father taking me onto the frozen lake in Coudenberg, when I was a small child. We attached blades to our shoes and skated around and around."

"Really?"

"Yes, it was something of which his mother, my grandmother, had been fond and she'd taught him." He smiled, as though going back in time. "Though apparently, Maximilian, my grandfather, he was not very good at it. Quite put out, in fact, that he couldn't do it the first time he tried."

"Habsburgs do like to be good at everything." She raised her eyebrows at him. "You will notice that with little Philip, if he doesn't master a song on the harpsichord or get the translation of Spanish to Portuguese right the first time, he gets very frustrated."

"It is not a bad trait. It means he will always be the best at everything he does." He leaned forward and took her hand. "I am aching to see my children, Isabella. When do they finish their lessons?"

"They will be finished by now. Dona will be giving them something to eat. I usually spend time with them after that."

"So I can go to them?"

"Yes." She nodded.

"Are you coming?"

"I am…" She closed her eyes and rested her head back on the chair
again. "I feel as though my strength has been sucked from me."

"Are you unwell?" He gripped her hand.

"No, I am quite well. But it has been a draining afternoon."

"I understand. And I am sorry again for my part in that."

"No more apologies, remember." She nodded to the door. "Go
and be with the children, enjoy them, and then come back to me. I will
be waiting for you."

"Are you sure?"

"I am sure." She paused. "On one condition."

"Anything, my love." He stood.

"You bathe before you step over that threshold again." She wrin-
kled her nose. "You smell of horses and dusty tracks."

He laughed. "Your wish is my command."

"It is, and don't forget it."

"Never, my empress." He stooped and kissed the back of her hand.
"And I promise I will atone for my mistakes. I will make you feel good
where you have felt bad, give you pleasure when you have known
sorrow. I will replace tears of grief with tears of ecstasy." He gazed at
her intently, sultry suggestion filling his eyes.

She gasped in a breath. Suddenly reminded, like a cannonball blast-
ing, of her husband's passionate promises and how good he was at
keeping them.

"You don't believe me?" he asked.

She cleared her throat. "I believe you."

"Good." He stood. "Rest and eat, for you will need your strength now that I am home and to be in your bed at night, each night, all night, starting on this one."

The deep timbre of his voice had her impatient for nightfall.

He turned and strode from the room, snatching up his belt and dagger as he went. His sword he left balanced against the wall.

The moment he'd left, Isabella rang the bell for Luisa.

She appeared only moments later. "Yes, Your Majesty?"

"I wish to have a plate of bread and cheese, olives and stuffed apples too. And when you have done that warm some water. I am going to bathe."

"Yes, Your Majesty." She nodded and disappeared.

Isabella stood and stretched her hands over her head. A strange sense of lightness tingled from her fingertips down to her toes. And it was as though a band had been taken from around her chest and breathing was easier. She was lighter. Her lungs filled easier. The knot in her shoulder had gone.

Was that because Charles was once again in the palace?

She suspected it was.

And she was going to enjoy every moment of him being at her side because goodness only knew when some other invasion or crisis would take him away.

She opened the chest of drawers beside her bed and moved several items around. There was nothing in there she wanted to wear when she received Charles. She'd taken to dressing for warmth, not to please her husband's gaze.

The door opened and Luisa returned. She held in her hand a package wrapped in white velvet and held secure with purple ribbon.

"What is that?" Isabella asked.

"The emperor asks me to give this to you."

"What is it?" She took it.

"A gift." Luisa smiled. "More than that, I do not know."

"How exciting." She set the package on the bed and gently tugged at the ribbon. It undid and she set it aside. Carefully, she opened the velvet. Within it she found folded, white satin, which she held up. It was a soft, loose gown of sorts and delicate lace decorated the neckline and short-capped sleeves.

"Goodness." She held it to her and saw that it reached the floor. "What a creation."

"I'd wager it is French," Luisa said, stroking the material between her thumb and fingers. "And of the finest quality."

"I would agree, though I am surprised my husband would purchase anything from France." She laughed softly. "Though perhaps he could not resist."

"I do not blame him. For what better gift for his wife who is also a queen and an empress?"

"He also gave me this." She pointed at the brooch.

Luisa paused to admire it. "How wonderfully unusual."

"Yes, it is a snowdrop flower."

Luisa smiled and left the room carrying the empty wine jug.

The gown was so very soft and the purest white, like snow. A little swirl of pleasure gripped Isabella. This was proof that even when they'd been apart Charles had thought of her fondly. He'd brought her gifts, personal gifts that he knew she'd like. He'd put thought into them.

She smiled and began to unlace the front of her gown. She'd bathe in rose water, have Luisa brush her hair one hundred times, and then dress in white, ready for her husband's attentions.

>>><<<

TWILIGHT STRETCHED OVER the city. For a magical moment, the rooftops were ablaze and then shadows stole the illusion into the night. All that remained were curling smoke lines drifting from chimneys into the bruised, lavender sky.

Isabella wore the gown Charles had given her. It was unlike anything she'd put on before—too sheer to be seen by any man other than
her husband. The outline of her breasts were clear to see and her
nipples small, dark disks protruding at the material. It grazed her hips
and if she smoothed from her abdomen downward, the bushy hair at
the junction of her thighs was easy to feel.

A candle had gone out on the windowsill, so she dipped a wooden
splint into the flames of the fire and re-lit it. Shadows danced around
the rose-scented room, and a tray had been set out with fortified wine,
grapes, and toasted hazelnuts and almonds.

She was ready for her husband and she hoped he would not be
long. After all of this time, it seemed the last few hours had been the
longest.

The door opened, a draft from the corridor sneaking in and cooling her ankles.

Charles filled the frame, broad shoulders and lean hips in silhouette for a moment before he ducked slightly and stepped into the
room.

"Did you enjoy your time with the children?" she asked, walking
to the wine.

"Yes. After I had reminded them who I was."

She laughed softly. "You should not be surprised."

"That is true. Their little memories are not as good as ours. But
they are wonderful children, with polite grace and fast minds. You
have done well with their education."

"I thank you for the compliment."

He stopped and ran his hand into his hair, causing it to stick up
messily. An action she'd seen a hundred times but not for so very long.
"You like your gown?" His attention dipped down her body, seeming
to caress her with each linger on her breasts, her hips, and then her
thighs. He lazily dragged it up again, as though completely unabashed
at his scrutiny.

The urge to squirm, or reach for a cape, held her hostage for a moment, then she reminded herself this was Charles. He'd seen her naked a hundred times.

That was how this gown made her feel. Naked.

"It is French?" she asked, turning and pouring wine.

He plucked an almond from the plate, tossed it in the air, and caught it in his mouth. "The gown?" he asked, after he'd swallowed. "Yes. It is from Northern France."

"And you like it on me?"

"Very much so."

Suddenly, he was behind her, his breath hot on her neck.

She gasped, his nearness sending lust shooting into her veins.

"On you it is," he whispered by her ear, "a perfect vision my fantasies will feed upon forevermore."

"Your fantasies?"

"Yes, my most secret desires that have kept me from going *loco* during our time apart. Thinking of you, imagining you with me. They are my fantasies."

"You did that?" She set the wine down and stared straight ahead, at the roaring fire.

"Yes." He kissed her neck, very gently. "Every night I thought of you as I went to sleep. Prayed for you and more."

"And more? I don't understand."

He rested his hands on her waist. "Much more."

"Tell me?"

"You. In my mind's eye, I saw you naked, legs spread, begging for me, on your knees taking my cock into your mouth. You, bathing, touching yourself—all of those images came to me."

"Charles...you... I..."

"And when they did"—he slid his hands upward to cup her breasts—"my cock hardened. It hardened and would not give me any relief. I had no choice but to ease the burden of it myself."

"You did that?"

"I did, too many times to count." He grazed his thumbs over her nipples. "And had I been a mere mortal, I would have repented my sins in confession, but I am Holy Roman Emperor and I absolve myself of sin." He kissed her neck again, his silky, smooth chin soft on her flesh. "I missed you so much, it hurt."

"You should not be in pain, my love. And if that...if touching yourself helped, God would understand."

"And you?" Gently, he turned her so she was facing him.

"Do I understand?"

"No. Did you touch yourself?"

"Charles, you cannot ask me such a thing." She rested her hands on his tunic and looked up at him.

"I can and I have. Tell me your answer."

She swept her tongue over her lips. "Then the answer is no. I do not have the uncomfortable appendage that you have, so there was no need, even though I missed you desperately."

"Ah, I see." He swept his hands down her back and squeezed her buttocks over the slippery material. "Do you mean this appendage?" He pulled her closer.

"Oh!" A flood of excitement filled her belly and her cunny tightened. "Yes, that is what I am referring to." His cock was as hard as stone behind his breeches.

He smiled, a confident, seductive smile that had her knees weakening. "It is time we both ended our years of aching for each other, don't you agree?"

"Yes." She went onto her tiptoes and kissed him gently.

But he quickly took control of the kiss, slipping his tongue in to find hers and running one hand to the nape of her neck to hold her in place.

She moaned softly as need gripped her.

And then he was tugging her to the bed. They fell onto it in a tangle of limbs, hands everywhere, pulling and tearing at clothing until they were naked.

"Love of my life," he murmured. "I need you so."

"As I need you."

She arched her back and speared her fingers into his hair as he took her left nipple into his mouth. He sucked and stroked it with his tongue as he palmed the underside. The sensations seemed to connect with her cunny and she pressed her thighs together, aware of herself dampening.

He switched breasts, leaving a trail with his tongue over her sternum.

She murmured his name and closed her eyes. If she hadn't felt so awake, so on fire with lust and bursting with love, she'd have thought she was dreaming.

"I need to remind myself," he said. "Of your taste."

He dotted kisses down her abdomen as he moved lower on the bed.

She parted her legs, knowing what he intended and happy for it. Her husband was so good with his tongue and oh, how she'd missed it.

"Roses," he murmured, placing his hands on her inner thighs. "Roses and love and all things female."

She curled her toes as he swept his tongue over her delicate folds. A tremble set up in her belly and she fisted the sheets.

He didn't preamble. He set to work on her nub. It came to life beneath his slick, stroking tongue, waking quickly from its dormant state. "Oh, yes…Charles."

He found her entrance and slipped one long finger into her.

She clamped around him, thrilling at the sensation of him being inside after all this time.

Within minutes, she was rising and bucking for more, her hips seeming to take on a life of their own. Her naked flesh tingled with longing and she was panting and gasping.

"Oh...oh...yes...just there...please, Charles." She threw her head back on the pillow and waited for the release that was almost there.

But then he stopped what he was doing.

"Charles!" Her eyes flew open and she glared at him.

He was looming over her, his erection directed at her cunny and his chest and arm muscles as solid as a cliff wall. "I want to be inside you when you find pleasure. I need to feel you around my cock."

As he'd said the word *cock*, he'd pushed into her. Not fast, but not slow, either.

She groaned and dug her nails into his biceps. "Oh, yes...more...more..."

"I forgot how demanding you are, Empress." He gave her a strained smile.

"So remember," she said, reaching for his buttocks. "Remember and give it to me."

His eyes narrowed and his jaw tensed. He thrust to full depth.

She cried out in bliss as his body connected with her nub. "Yes. Like that." She canted up to meet him, grinding against him as he pulled out and shoved back in. "Yes, like that. Like that. Oh, don't stop."

"Not. Stopping." He was like a wild animal riding into her. Humping. Panting. Sweating.

She took it all. She needed it all. Very quickly, her pleasure was there, a huge ball of tension that needed to be set free. To overflow. To burst from her.

She held her breath and stared up at his face. Their eyes connected and she was sure she could see right into the very depths of who he was, his soul, his bare bones.

But then it could be contained no longer and ecstasy gripped her. It spread from her cunny to every corner of her body. She shook and clenched and wailed in bliss.

Charles found his release, several powerful thrusts that had the air shunting from her lungs.

Another delicious wave of pleasure washed over her, seeming to take over her entire body in a series of spasms.

"Oh, good Lord above." Charles dipped his head and kissed her.

She clung to him, thankful her husband was such a talented and skilled lover.

"I missed you so much," she murmured against his lips when he'd slowed then stilled.

"What exactly did you miss about me?" he asked with a devilish grin.

"I missed…" She paused and pushed a lock of hair from near his eye. "Every inch of you."

CHAPTER EIGHTEEN

"'IT IS ANNOUNCED,'" Charles stated, reading from a scroll sent to him by Eustace Chapuys, his imperial ambassador stationed in England, "'that Henry of England has a new daughter.'"

Isabella looked up from where she was pressing flowers with Maria. "That's his second daughter, is it not?" She passed a cornflower to Maria, who carefully spread out the petals on a sheet of parchment that was already covered with many others.

"Yes, his second. Elizabeth she is to be named." He paused. "I bet he wishes it were a son." He resisted adding that the pompous king would have been spitting dust at the news of a girl.

"Sons and daughters are both blessings. We should remember that." Isabella kissed Maria on the top of her head. Their daughter didn't seem to notice and carried on concentrating on the flowers.

"Naturally." Charles sipped on his honeyed tea. "Though if he were to legitimize Henry Fitzroy, he would have a son of nearly ruling age."

"I am surprised he hasn't, for he has given him titles."

"This is true." Charles shrugged. "In any case, now he has a daughter whom he will no doubt go to great pains to marry into our family, thinking it will give him power in Europe." He glanced at Philip, who was playing with a set of wooden soldiers and horses Alvaro had made for him. "I am sure we will hear from the King of England soon on that front."

"And what will you say?"

"If it were his first daughter, the one he so wanted me to wait around for…" As if that was ever going to have happened. "Then perhaps."

"Mary?"

"Yes, if it were Mary," Charles said, "I would be in agreement, her mother, Catherine, our aunt, is a good Catholic, but this one, with this new wife…" He huffed. "I am reluctant."

"Why?"

Charles thought for a moment. "I believe it is she who has encouraged Henry to disrespect the pope with all her pressing for England to be free from Rome." He paused, the word *heresy* feeling dirty on his tongue.

"Queen Anne Boleyn?"

"Yes, she." He nodded. "I knew her once." He set the scroll aside and walked to the fire, tossing on a log. Sparks danced upward. "When I was a boy."

"You did? You never told me."

"No, I have not thought of it for many years." His mind drifted back to living with his dear Aunt Margaret in Mechelan. A young Anne had visited, stayed for several seasons, if he remembered correctly. She'd been bright of mind but outspoken. Well-mannered but with an edge of rebellion.

He remembered one night her talking about Martin Luther and his journey of seven hundred miles over the Alps and down the spine of Italy. How when the young priest had arrived in Rome he'd been dismayed by the Church's extravagance and corruption, and its lack of interest in the plight of the poor. She'd become animated, accusing the Church of thinking itself as powerful as God.

"You appear vexed, husband," Isabella said, standing and walking to him. She stroked his hair, trying to flatten a few strands that seemed intent on sticking up of late.

"When Chapuys wrote to me some time ago, he said she was more Lutheran than Luther himself."

"And you believed him?" Isabella's eyes widened. "That is quite an accusation."

"I have no reason not to trust him. And because of what has happened since." He shrugged, though his brow creased. "It is a truth."

Isabella shook her head and helped herself to a slice of cheese. She stood beside the fire. "It is strange times we live in, with much change in every track of the compass."

"I am all for change in the right direction." He shook his head. "But breaking away from Rome, that will be Henry's downfall."

"His downfall?" Philip suddenly looked up from his toys. "What do you mean, Father? What is a downfall?"

"I mean..." Charles plucked up a bunch of grapes. He tossed one into the air and caught it in his mouth. "That he has done something bad, that things will happen because of it that cause him to fall down."

"What, like the soldiers will come for him?" Philip's eyes widened. "And knock him over?"

"Yes, something like that. Once they have journeyed over the sea to England, that is."

"Then an armada would be better if there is sea to cross." Philip reached for a wooden galleon. It was a toy he'd been given recently and liked to float on the gardens' fountains. "An armada of Spanish ships, loaded with cannons, flags and sails, lots of guns and swords and—"

"Yes, yes, that is enough." Isabella laughed. "Here, eat some grapes. Soon it will be time for your walk with Dona." She passed both children little sprigs of grapes. "And you may take your galleon, Philip, and play with it on the water."

"May I pick some more pink flowers?" Maria asked. "I don't have enough."

"Of course, as many as you need. This is going to be a beautiful flower picture, my sweetness." Isabella smiled and unfolded the crease from a tiny, white petal.

Charles watched his wife. He was constantly amazed by her. She could switch from wise ruler to gentle mother to giving lover from one heartbeat to the next. He hated himself for leaving her for so long. He never would had he known how she'd suffered without him. He vowed never to do so again, though with things constantly simmering around his empire, it would only be a matter of time until he would have to leave her as his regent and pay attention to defense.

"We should have a celebratory feast," he said suddenly.

"We should?" She studied him, a smile tickling her lips. "And what is the occasion?"

"You said had you known I was returning, you'd have organized such an event."

"That is true."

"And it never happened." He reached for her and slid his hands around her narrow waist. "I feel cheated out of my feast."

"You have feasted plenty since you returned." She laughed and set her hands on his chest.

"It is true. I enjoy the Spanish food immensely. It tastes of sunshine." He touched his lips to hers in a soft, sweeping kiss. "But let us celebrate with our friends."

"It is a good idea."

He was pleased she was approving. "And Bishop Gabriel, it is his first time here in Spain. Let us show him how we revel. There are many dishes for him to try. Music for him to hear, dances to learn. Don't you agree?"

"I certainly do. When do you wish for this feast?"

"As soon as possible. How about tomorrow?"

"I can set cook to the task and Alvaro will choose a pig for the table."

"Alvaro?"

"Yes, he always chooses the pig, and he is good at it."

"I can choose the pig." Charles tapped his chest. "It is my feast. It should be me."

"Very well. You choose the pig. Just make sure it is good and fat as well as healthy. Be sure to check its trotters."

"I can do that." And he would because this was the third thing his wife had claimed Alvaro would do because he was so good at it. Much as he liked his old friend, he feared he had rather stepped into his shoes while he'd been away seeing to imperial matters.

Isabella picked up a small, brass bell. She rang it, the sound echoing around the room. "You know you are likely to receive welcome home gifts."

"I am not opposed to gifts." He shrugged. "Are you?"

"No. I find them exquisite, and quite interesting, especially if they are from countries to which I have never been." She lifted a small cloak from the back of a chair. "Philip, come and put this on to go outside with Dona."

Charles walked to the window and looked out at the courtyard, his mind going back to Isabella in the beautiful, white, satin gown he'd brought her from France. She had been a vision in it. All of his dreams come true.

Leaning his hands on the sill, he beat down a wave of heat in his groin. Their first few nights back together had been incredible. Worth the wait...almost. She was so responsive and open to him, her body seeming to join with his as though God had made them for each other and no one else.

Dona's voice was behind him now, shooing the children out with boats and books, boots and cloaks. Isabella was overseeing proceedings.

When the room went quiet he turned.

Isabella was pouring wine beside the fire, the light of the flame flashing through the glass decanter.

"Alvaro," he said, folding his arms. He had to have this conversation. It was irritating him like an annoying mosquito bite. "What does he mean to you?"

"I beg your pardon?" She looked up, surprise widening her eyes.

"Alvaro. He is always at your side and you mention him first when there are things to be done." He stepped up to her. "Things to be done by your husband."

"I do not know what you are getting at." She frowned, picked up her wine, and sipped.

"I think you do." He couldn't help the sharpness in his voice.

"Mm, perhaps I do." She bit on her bottom lip. "But I am choosing to ignore it, Charles." Like his voice, there was a note of irritation in hers. Irritation…or was it a note of warning?

He chose to ignore it. "When you are not in your private chambers he is never more than a few feet from you. Indeed, it was his face I saw next to yours on my arrival at court just days ago. Up at the window."

She kept her gaze steadily on him and sipped her wine.

"And just then," he went on, "you suggested Alvaro to choose the feasting pig. And yesterday, he poured you wine and yet none for me. He passed you the figs and spices—no one else. And later on, when there was—"

"Stop!" She held up her hand. "Stop this now."

He frowned and opened his mouth again.

"I am not jesting, Charles," she said quickly. "You stop this right now because I know what you are doing."

"What am I doing?" He reached for his wine, took a gulp, then set it down with a bang. A drip sloshed over the side and trickled down the stem to form a puddle on the tray.

"You are being jealous. Jealous of the man you left behind to take care of me while you were gone. And now you are bitter because he did just that."

"I am here now! *I* will take care of you. That is my duty when I am in residence at court."

She pressed her lips together. It was a gesture that severely unnerved him and he didn't know why when he'd faced battles and waded through torrents of icy water, scaled mountains and beaten an angry viper from his tent only a week ago.

"You will stop this," she said firmly. "Alvaro is a loyal servant who has, as you said, been at my side for many years while you have been away. And that was your instruction to him. To do just that."

"Yes, I instructed him to be your servant, not to look at you as though there were no other women alive on God's Earth. To tend to you as if no one else were in the room, not even the emperor himself." He paused, sucking in a breath. "He has never taken a wife and I think I know why."

"Pray tell." She set down her wine. Again, she crossed her arms and her lips pursed.

"I think he is in love with you." There, he'd said it. "He is in love." He pointed at her. "With you."

"And would that be a bad thing?" She cocked her head. "For a servant to love his empress?"

Charles frowned.

"Don't you think that just makes him better at his job?" she said. "Better at caring for me in your absence? This is a dangerous, changing world in which we live. He stood in your place as protector of the head of the realm. You cannot condemn a man for being loyal and diligent." She paused. "Am I right?"

"If he has only ever acted as a servant should." His jaw tensed.

"If you are asking if he has ever acted in a way that could be considered inappropriate, then no, he hasn't. His conduct has always been impeccable." She narrowed her eyes.

"But...I...I just want to—"

"Think very carefully about what you say next, Charles. What you ask next. You might not be able to take it back once it has passed your lips."

He wanted to ask if Alvaro had ever tried to kiss her. If he'd touched her in any way that was less than gentlemanly.

He wanted to ask if Alvaro had seduced his wife, the empress, during the long, lonely nights in the depths of winter or in the heady afternoon heat of summer.

But the glint in Isabella's eyes kept his words firmly in his mouth. As she'd said, he wouldn't be able to take them back if he accused her of adultery. When they were uttered that would be it. He'd have to follow through with his belief.

And that would mean losing his wife.

And if he accused Alvaro of behaving inappropriately, he'd have no choice but to have him hanged at dawn.

"Good," Isabella said. "I see you have returned to using your usual wisdom and good sense on this matter, Charles."

He cleared his throat.

"So we will speak of it no more." She walked up to him and reached for his hand. She drew it to her mouth and kissed his ring. "For we promised ourselves, before God, to each other all of that time ago and it is a promise neither of us has broken."

She looked into his eyes, seeming to see the turmoil in his mind. "And I love you, with everything that I am. And that goes for if you are in my bed or in another country. That love doesn't change. It stays the same. Strong and true and devoted." She leaned in and touched her lips to his, her sweet breath lacing his lips. "You have always been the only man for me, and you always will be the only man for me."

He tucked a strand of hair behind her ear, slotting it next to her small, black headdress. "Forgive me for my foolish words."

"You were lucky. You didn't say anything that can't be forgiven."

He smiled, relieved that he had such a benevolent wife. "It is complicated for a man to have such a beautiful wife as you. I want in part to show you off to the world but also keep you hidden, for my eyes only."

"Well, some of me is for your eyes only." She laughed softly.

"That is true." He yanked her close, pulling her chest against his. "And perhaps it is siesta time now." He slanted his mouth over hers and kissed her.

For a moment, she kissed him back, but then she pushed him away, laughing once again. "Perhaps a little later, but as you have just ordered an emperor's feast for tomorrow, there are things I must do. Preparations must get underway."

"They can wait." He snuggled his face against her soft neck.

"No." She wriggled. "They cannot wait, but *you* must, Emperor." She grinned and turned away. "But it will be worth the wait. You know that to be true."

He groaned and watched her leave the room. It seemed no matter his vast lands and imperial power, his titles, and lineage, his sweet, little wife always managed to assert her authority in some way.

CHAPTER NINETEEN

ISABELLA SURVEYED THE extravagantly adorned feasting table. The guests had yet to arrive and servants were rushing around adding more loaded plates to the spread, pouring wine into ornate jugs, and lighting silver candelabras.

At the center of the table were the two suckling pigs Charles had picked out. They had rosy apples in their mouths and were surrounded by roast chestnuts and figs. Plates of sweet rolls, codfish, and chopped spinach were dotted around, and steaming meat casseroles were set over the fire to keep warm.

"The bread is good," Isabella said, nodding at a stack of fresh loaves that smelled divine. "As is the Manchego." She broke off a piece of the hard cheese to nibble.

"I am glad you approve, Your Majesty," Cook said. "The cheese is from a local farm."

"I approve heartily. You and your staff must have worked through the night to prepare all of this."

"Yes, Your Majesty, we did."

"And I thank you all for your service. It will be remembered when wages are delivered at the end of the month."

"I thank you." Cook bobbed her head, her soft chin wobbling. "Is there anything else I can add?"

"You appear to have thought of everything." Isabella turned at the sound of a lute string being plucked. "That will be all, and ensure the staff and their families get a meal from the leftovers."

"They will be grateful for that."

Isabella looked at the vast, arched windows in the banqueting room. It was dark outside and soon carriages would arrive with hungry guests looking forward to an evening of entertainment with the emperor and empress.

"Your Majesty," Luisa said. "You should dress for the celebrations."

"You are right." She took one last glance around then swept from the room.

Luisa followed.

"Are the children in bed?"

"Yes, Dona has seen to them."

"Good. I will bid them goodnight and then prepare. Do you have my new scarlet gown laid out?"

"Yes, Your Majesty."

"And I will wear my mother's cream, lace headdress. The one with the pearls sewn into it."

"I have that ready for you. Excellent choice. It will complement the gown perfectly."

⤜⤛⤛

IT TOOK TWO hours for Isabella to ready herself for the banquet. But when Charles entered her chambers to escort her downstairs she knew it had been worth the effort.

"My love," he said, holding her hands and looking her up and down. "You are a vision."

"I am glad you approve."

"I do, very much so." He smiled. "You will be twice as beautiful as every other woman in the room."

"And I'd wager you will be twice as handsome as every other man in the room." She let her attention drift down his body. He wore shiny, black boots, white breeches, and a brown, leather belt with a brass buckle and a dagger hanging from it. His tunic was heavily embroidered with gold stitching depicting the Habsburg coat of arms and had balled sleeves. Over it, he wore a ruby-red cloak, fur-lined and so soft, it seemed to shine in the candlelight.

"I had my hair cut," he said, removing his beret.

"About time." She smiled and ran her hair through the now short strands. "You were looking quite piratical."

He laughed. "I will allow you, and only you, to say such a thing."

"Your Majesty." Luisa was at Isabella's side. "Would you like to wear your new brooch?" She offered forward the snowdrop.

"I will not." She waved it away.

"I thought you liked it," Charles said.

"I do very much. But I expect we will receive gifts and if anyone is kind enough to gift me a brooch, I will put it on there and then as a sign of my appreciation."

"You are so very thoughtful." He kissed her cheek. "Shall we go and greet our esteemed guests?"

"We should."

The banqueting hall was a hum of conversation when they arrived. Guests milled around with goblets of fine wine and music played softly in the corner.

"Lords, ladies, and gentlemen," Alvaro called upon seeing Isabella and Charles in the doorway, "please welcome your hosts, the Holy Roman Emperor, King of Spain, Archduke of Austria, Charles of Habsburg, and his wife, the Holy Roman Empress, Queen of Spain, and Princess of Portugal, Isabella."

The room had become utterly silent. All eyes turned their way. Two guards banged the bases of their pikes on the wooden floor four times, and then Isabella and Charles stepped into the room.

Isabella kept her arm linked with Charles's as she took wine from a servant. She then smiled greetings, nodded hello, and tipped her head in acknowledgement as they walked through the crowd, who parted for them.

The room was warm and smelled of herbs, hot broth, and spice. When she sat on her throne, beside Charles, her stomach rumbled and she realized she was looking forward to the feast as much as everyone else.

"Your Majesties," Gabriel said, appearing before them and bowing deeply. "It is with great honor that I am received here as one of your humble and loyal guests."

"We are happy to have you," Isabella said. "My husband speaks very highly of you and appreciates your candor and wisdom."

"I hope I do not overstep the mark with my frankness." Gabriel looked at Charles.

"On the contrary, there are very few people who are utterly frank with me. It is refreshing." He reached for Isabella's hand and turned to her. "And it reminds me not to let my thoughts be the only opinions to consider."

She smiled at him. "It is a wise ruler who can listen as well as speak."

He lifted her hand to his mouth and kissed her knuckles. His lips were warm and soft.

"I would like to offer the empress this gift," Gabriel said, holding forward a blue, velvet box. "If the emperor will allow it."

"And does this gift have significance?" Charles asked.

Isabella frowned slightly, unused to such a question from her husband.

"My love, Gabriel has thought behind everything he does." Charles gestured to his friend. "It is one of the things I like the most about him."

"Indeed, it does have significance." Gabriel offered the box farther forward. "It was my mother's. She will be smiling down from heaven if she sees a woman as beautiful as the empress wearing it."

"Oh, how wonderful." Isabella smiled. "Please show it to me."

Gabriel flicked open the lid and revealed a brooch. It was a fish, made of gold and the head and scales a deep red.

"It does not have precious stones and is not of the value of your other jewelry," Gabriel said. "But I hope you will find it amusing, if nothing else."

"Yes, it is so unusual." Isabella took the box. "I have never seen anything like it."

Gabriel grinned. "My father had it made for her, many years ago, in Milan."

"It is all the way from Milan." She took it and passed it to Charles. "I do love things from faraway places such as this."

"How extraordinary." Charles studied it. "A fish."

"Can you put it on, please?" Isabella tapped just above her right breast.

Charles stood and came before her. Very gently, he attached it. "A charming gift indeed, Gabriel." He smiled and sat. "We thank you."

"As I thank you for bringing me here with you." Gabriel bowed low then stepped back.

An old nobleman, Juan Gomez, approached holding a wicker basket that appeared heavy. "Your Majesties," he said, setting the basket down. "I bring you gifts."

"We thank you," Charles said. "What is it?" He nodded at a servant, who lifted back the white muslin covering the contents of the basket.

"Honey," Juan said. "Lavender honey, collected from my brother's hives. He also grows lavender and you will taste it in the bees' honey. They collect the nectar from the lavender fields."

"Really?" Isabella leaned forward. "I would never have thought such a thing."

"It is a fact, and I hope, Empress, it will be to your liking on bread and in tea."

"I am sure it will be because I like both honey and lavender." She smiled. "We thank you."

He bowed low and backed away.

The servant quickly removed the basket.

The wife of a general stepped forward. She was petite, her gown the color of buttermilk, and her hair was not far off the shade of a carrot.

"Adriana, we welcome you," Charles said. "And we wish Santiago a speedy recovery from his illness."

"He gains strength every day since he is returned from his travels."

"That is good to hear," Isabella said. "Please ensure you take some food home for him."

"I will, Empress, I thank you." She curtseyed. "And please accept this gift." She handed Isabella a small package wrapped in black silk.

It felt like a bottle of some sort and Isabella unwrapped it. Sure enough, it was a small, glass bottle filled with pale, glossy liquid. A skinny, black ribbon had been tied around the neck of the bottle.

"It is to drink?" Charles asked.

"No. No." She shook her head and came a little closer, lowering her voice. "It is one of a set Santiago picked up on his travels. It is not to be indigested, you understand."

"We understand," Charles said.

"So what is it for?" Isabella asked. "The animals?"

Adriana giggled. "Not exactly. It is for you." She held her hands out and made a slow circle. "It is for your skin, to make it soft and smooth and slippery. To rub and knead tiredness and aches from the body. It can go everywhere, and it smells of petals."

Charles reached for it. "It is not water?" He tipped it this way and that. It seemed to cling to the side of the bottle.

"No, it is oil for the body. I hope you will enjoy it." She didn't wait for an answer and backed away with her head bowed.

Charles leaned toward Isabella, an impish grin playing with his lips. "I am sure we will," he whispered. "This is most intriguing."

Isabella ignored him, though a tingle of heat went up her spine. Oil that went *everywhere*?

Several more gifts were presented. They included a fine, lace shawl, a bottle of excellent fortified wine, a cushion with a golden, two-headed eagle embroidered onto it, and a gun case made of the finest oak.

"Are you hungry, my love?" Charles asked her.

"Very. And so are our guests."

He nodded and stood. "Our cherished guests," he said loudly, "we thank you for your company and now, please, let us eat and drink and be merry."

Isabella looked at the small crowd. There was a pause, just to be sure Charles had finished speaking, and then the conversation and hustle for plates and feast began.

Luisa appeared before her with a tray of food. "Your Majesty. I prepared your favorites."

"Ah, you are so thoughtful, I thank you." Isabella took the tray. It contained two plates, a small one with bread, butter, and honey, and another with ham, figs, pickled eggs, and spinach.

"May I get you anything else?" Luisa asked.

"No, thank you. Be sure to eat yourself."

"I will."

Charles also had food delivered by a senior servant. "Cook has excelled herself," he said, "and on such short notice."

"It is certainly a room of happy people."

There was laughter and chatter, and the scrape of knives and forks on plates. The music played and the fire crackled.

Isabella had a lovely sense of contentment. Here, in her home, all was well. Her children were upstairs asleep under the watchful eye of Dona. Charles was at her side. And there were guards at the doors, and loyal friends enjoyed themselves all around her.

It was certainly something she could get used to.

When she'd finished eating the tray was taken by a servant. She sat quietly and sipped on fortified wine.

"Soon we will dance," Charles said.

"We will?"

"Yes, the only question is: Will it be a Low Country dance or Spanish?"

"Spanish, my love, for that is where we are." She laughed.

"Some of the people here miss home. Perhaps the Carol?"

"I'd rather not. It is dreary in comparison."

"In comparison to your stamping and clacking." He laughed.

"Do not let your mother hear you say that." She raised her eyebrows. "The story of Princess Joanna performing flamenco in French court when she visited is still being talked about."

"Ah, yes, you are right about that." He kissed her hand. "As usual."

They sat for a few minutes and then when it appeared the guests had finished eating, Charles nodded at the musician.

He stopped playing.

Charles stood, turned to Isabella, and urged her to stand with him.

She did, wondering why the music had stopped.

The hum of conversation quieted and as they walked off the podium onto the wooden floor of the banqueting room, people stepped back to give them space. "Gentle noble folk," Charles said, instantly commanding everyone's attention, "I present to you my wife, Empress Isabella."

There was a gentle ripple of applause.

"Isn't she exquisite?" he said, smiling at her. "Isn't she the most beautiful woman to have ever walked on God's Earth? The heavens were smiling the day she came into the world, and the angels rejoiced."

"Yes, Your Majesty," a few people murmured. "Beautiful."

He walked around her, gently trailing his fingertip over her shoulder and across her nape.

A delicate tremor went over her skin. "Charles?" she said, starting to turn to him. "What are you—?"

"No, my love." He kept her in place with a slight pressure on her back. "Let your people admire you, for you are the closest thing to a goddess they will ever lay their eyes upon."

He stood before her again, his hand wrapped around hers. "And let it be known," he said, sweeping his attention around the room, "that the empress is mine and mine alone. This queen is *my* wife." He tapped his chest. "To be touched by no other man."

Isabella's breath hitched. Was he referring to their earlier conversation? She sought out Alvaro, who stood by the door.

His broad-brimmed hat shadowed his face and he held a pewter goblet. As usual, he was a few steps away from the crowd. She often wondered if he felt he didn't quite fit in at court. There was something a little wild and outdoors about him. A tamed animal who could turn feral again if the mood struck him.

"You all know that as emperor, I travel often," Charles went on. "Being King of Christendom requires these sacrifices from me and I am happy to give that to God and to Christ Our Savior, but..." He paused, sucking in a breath. "But while I expect my wife to be adored, tended to, and protected during my absences, I trust that everyone knows the boundaries."

"Your Majesty," an old clergyman said with a frown. "Your wife is a good Catholic and is surrounded by such. You have no fears."

"Any man with a wife as beautiful and intelligent as mine has fears." Charles's voice was a deep rumble. "Wouldn't you agree?"

"Yes, yes, Your Majesty." The bishop lowered his gaze to the ground. "Accept my apology."

It was clear Charles was determined to have this very public conversation.

Though was it directed to anyone in particular?

Of course it was.

Isabella curled her toes in her shoes and pursed her lips. There had never been anything improper between her and Alvaro. He loved her deeply, she knew that. He showed it in his actions. It made him a loyal and constant support when she was a woman ruling on her own. But she didn't want him in her bed, or in her heart. That was something she wouldn't entertain. Her devotion to Charles was absolute. Always had been and always would be.

"So I will say this," Charles said, holding up his hand. He flicked his attention to the doorway, to Alvaro. "Any man harboring desires for my wife should either keep them locked deep inside forever, or leave not just this city, but also Spain and the wider empire. Because if I ever, ever find out that someone has indecent thoughts about my wife, seedy ambitions, hopes for clandestine liaisons, they will be hanging from the portcullis by morn, guts spilling to the ground for the rats to feast upon."

Isabella gulped. What a horrible image. "My love," she whispered. "Please."

He turned to her. His eyes flashed. "Do not upset yourself, my love." He kissed her cheek. "And forgive me for saying what needed to be said. For how can I punish a crime that has not been defined as such, by me, the emperor? Everyone must know how I feel about you. You are my one true love and it would be a dagger to my heart should someone try to steal you away."

"No one is going to steal me away." She touched his cheek. "You are also my one true love, which means we can never be parted." She smiled softly. "We were apart for many years, Charles, with never so much as a glance at another. That has to tell you something."

"It does. It tells me I want it to stay that way."

CHAPTER TWENTY

THE FEASTING AND dancing went on late into the night. As the clock struck midnight, a juggler performed a breathtaking show of catch with blazing sticks. The crowd gasped and applauded at his daring.

"My love," Charles said, "I wish to steal you away."

"You do?"

"Yes, there is something I wish to show you." He tugged her to the left and they slipped behind a thick, red curtain.

"Charles?"

He grinned—the grin he gave her when he was up to something or when he had a secret he was about to share.

"You have me intrigued."

"As was my plan." He took her hand and opened a small, wooden door that the servants used to be discreet when coming and going from the banqueting room. "Come this way."

"Where are we going?" She had never been along the corridor he was now urging her through. It was shadowy, with squat candles in hollowed recesses. The floor was stone and the walls bereft of artwork.

"You will soon see." He laughed softly. "And you will like it."

"I hope so."

She followed him up a narrow set of stairs, then along another hallway, and more stairs. Then the air grew a fraction cooler and the candlelight gave way to the thick dark of a moonless night.

"Careful where you step," Charles said, cupping her elbow. "We are high up."

A narrow doorway led them outside into the Spanish night.

"Where are we?" she asked, stopping and letting her eyes adjust to the darkness.

"The highest point of the palace," he said. "Somewhere only the chimney sweeps go."

"You think me a chimney sweep?"

He laughed, a soft, milky sound, and came to stand behind her. Wrapping his arms around her waist, he slotted his body up against hers. "No, I think you are a stargazer, or at least you will be." He kissed the side of her head tenderly. "Look up."

She did and immediately caught her breath. She was used to the night sky, but tonight with no moon, the stars were vivid, like a million gossamer stitches sewn into rich, black velvet.

"Can you see them?"

"The stars? Yes, there are so many. Everywhere you look."

"Yes."

"And when I see a black dark patch"—she stared at an area straight ahead—"they seem to just appear, winking at first and then oh... What...What is that?" Something had streaked across the sky, a flash of white, like an arrow being fired. It was quickly followed by another and another.

Charles laughed and held her tighter. "You are surprised?"

"I have seen perhaps one or two streaks of light in the night sky before, but look..." Her eyes tracked the sky. "There are so many. And they are so fast."

"They are the tears of Saint Lawrence."

"Saint Lawrence?" She cast her mind back to her theological teachings. "The Christian martyr who was killed by the Romans?"

"The very one."

"I cannot remember the story exactly."

"My clever wife cannot remember." He squeezed her to him. There was a teasing tone in his voice. "Surely, you can."

"I cannot remember all of the taxes, treaties, and orders I must give to rule as regent and then, on top of that, remember every single Bible story in detail."

"Do not pout." He kissed her neck. "And though it is dark, I know you are doing so."

She resisted the urge to huff.

"You will remember when I tell you," Charles said softly, his breath warm on her ear. "Saint Lawrence was a martyr, as you said. Ordered to death by the Emperor Valerian, along with many other members of the Roman clergy. He was the last of the seven deacons of Rome to die."

Isabella listened quietly, watching the streaks showering through the sky above her and imagining them as the poor saint's tears.

"When he was summoned before the executioners, Lawrence was ordered to bring all the wealth of the Church with him," Charles went on. "He showed up with a handful of crippled, poor, and sick men, and when questioned, replied that the men were the true wealth of the Church."

"Yes, of course, I recall now." She rested her hands on Charles's forearms as they held her around the waist. "Poor man, he was cooked on a gridiron, wasn't he?"

"Yes, and it is said that his last words were a jest."

"A jest? It is no laughing matter, surely, being cooked alive." She turned within his arms and looked up at him.

"I would agree wholeheartedly. I should thoroughly hate to be cooked, but legend has it he quipped to his killers, 'Turn me over, I'm done on this side.'"

Isabella gasped. "Charles, what a thing to say of a saint. Of a Christian martyr."

He laughed and held her close. "I am only repeating what I heard."

"And who told you such a thing?"

"Does it matter?"

"Yes, I want to know if this is how men talk."

"It was Gabriel. On our journey here, over the mountains." He swept his lips over hers. "Do not be so shocked. For here we remember Saint Lawrence's sacrifice. God has put his tears in the sky for all to see."

"I am shocked of such talk, yes." She ran her hand over his hair, enjoying his new, shorter style. "I am now also wondering what other things you men talk of in the dead of the night when you are all weary from riding and in the mountains, or on the plains, or sitting around the fire with wine." She paused. "When there are no women to regulate your tongues."

He tipped his head. "I do not know what you mean."

"I think you do." She smiled and cupped his cheeks. "Emperor of mine. Your mind is too lively to be still for long, much like your body."

"That is true, and yes, I am yours. As you are mine." He lowered his face to hers and whispered, "If that is all I ever am, your husband, from this moment on in my life, I would die a happy man."

"Do not talk of dying." Her heart squeezed with love. "I could not bear it."

"As I could not bear it if I were to lose you." He narrowed his eyes. "Sometimes I pray that it will be I who goes first, for I could not breathe in a world in which you are not."

"Oh, Charles." She went onto her toes and kissed him. "And I couldn't live without you. God blessed us indeed when he aligned our paths."

Charles took control of the kiss, slanting his head and finding her tongue with his. He tasted of wine and figs and of *him*. His unique taste that she craved when they were parted but never forgot.

He ran his hands to her behind, cupping her buttocks over her gown. "I believe it is time for bed." He pulled her closer still.

"You are tired?" she asked quietly with her fingers linked at the back of his neck. She was enjoying the length of his body pressed against hers.

"No, my love. I simply wish to be in bed, with you...naked."

She giggled. "But what about our guests?"

"They are bloated with food, pickled with wine. They will not notice we are gone."

She thought of Luisa and Alvaro, her constant companions. They would have already noticed her absence. "But what about—?"

"Do not worry," Charles said. "I gave word to Gabriel that we were leaving the festivities." He paused. "You are with me, my love. There is nothing with which to concern yourself."

"Yes, yes, I am with you." She sighed contentedly. "And I am not worried. Never when I am with you."

"Good, then let us bid goodnight to Saint Laurence and his falling tears and navigate our way to our bedchamber." He released her waist and took her hand.

"Can you find it? The servants' passages are a maze."

"I found my way from the Low Countries to England to Italy, Vienna, and then to Spain and many more places between, my love, so yes, I can find the way to our bedchamber. Do not fear."

She giggled again, enjoying his jovial mood. And she was glad not to be going back to the banquet. The appetite she'd had for food had been satisfied. Now there was another appetite that required sating.

Charles did indeed find his way back to their bedchamber, and when they stepped inside he shooed out one of the palace cats that had settled herself on their bed, then slipped the lock on the door.

She raised an eyebrow at him.

"I do not wish to be disturbed," he said.

"The servants have been and gone." She pointed to their gifts, which had been set on a long table beneath the window.

"Ah, yes." Charles picked up a poker and nudged a log on the fire. He then threw another on. "That must be how the cat sneaked in."

"It is really so hot," Isabella said, removing her headdress. "Do we need the log?"

"You are about to be devoid of clothes, my love." He balanced the poker back in its tall, iron stand. "So I am sure you'll want the room warm."

"Is that right?" A little twist of excitement swirled in her belly and her arms ached to hold her husband close against her flesh, no clothes between them.

"It is the *only* thing that is going to happen next..." He paused and picked up the bottle of oil they'd been given. "And this..."

"The oil?"

"Yes." He removed the stopper and inhaled. "It is sweet."

"May I?"

He stepped up to her and held it beneath her nose.

The scent of roses hit her. "Oh, it is lovely, like flowers on a summer's day."

"Yes." He bit on his bottom lip and appeared to hold in a grin. "And apparently, it is for working into the flesh, muscles, and tendons, and it can go everywhere." He reached for the bow on her gown and tugged, loosening the material that covered her breasts. "So shall we try it out?"

"Are you asking permission, husband?"

"Not really." He chuckled. "We *will* try it out."

He placed the oil beside the bed then cupped her face in his hands. His eyes bore into hers for a moment, then he kissed her with gentle passion.

She clung to his arms and melted against him. Her tongue found his and the rest of the palace, the city, the world faded away. They were alone together. That was all she needed.

As they kissed, he roamed her body, tugging at her bodice, her sleeves, and then loosening her hair from its grips. Her hair quickly tumbled down, as did the top of her gown.

"I will never get enough of you," he said, cupping her naked right breast. "Not for as long as I live."

"And I you, my love." She pushed at his cloak and it fell to the floor with a soft *whump*. "For when we are together my soul is content."

"God has entwined our souls. We will never be apart in this life or the next."

"That is my hope." With a few gentle tugs, she released his tunic from his waistband. "Take this off."

He released her for a second, gripped the tunic in his fist, between his shoulder blades, and dragged it over his head. His hat tumbled to the side and he let his tunic land on top of it.

She set her hand over his sternum, the soft hairs there tickling her palm. The cross he wore around his neck glinted in the candlelight.

"My body craves yours," he said, his voice low and seductive.

"So give in to the craving." She pushed at the last of her clothes, the skirt of her gown landing around her ankles.

As Charles tugged at his belt, his gaze roamed her body, his pupils were wide, and a sheen of moisture sat on his lips from where he'd just run his tongue over them.

"You are slow," she said, jutting her hip to the left and placing her hands on her waist.

"I intend to take my time. Savor you."

"I like the sound of that."

He pushed at his breeches, then stooped to remove them and his boots. When he unfolded to his full height his cock protruded hard and long.

"Come. This way." He led her to the bed. "Lie down, on your stomach."

"On my stomach?"

"Yes, I wish to work out the knot in your shoulder. The one I saw you rubbing earlier."

"I am sure it is gone."

"Not quite, and best to be sure."

"You want to treat it with the oil?"

"Yes, with the oil." He nodded at the bed. "I promise it will be good."

"You have never let me down yet."

She crawled onto the bed, knowing full well his attention was on her behind as she did so. The sheets were cool as she lay down, her breasts pressing on the soft material and her head sinking into the feather pillow.

It felt strange to be like this, intimate yet distanced. But only for a second because then he straddled her hips, his warm, hard body touching hers gently—his balls, inner thighs, cock.

"Are you ready?" he whispered.

"Yes." She closed her eyes.

But she quickly opened them when a cool drizzle hit the flesh over her spine. It trickled to the hollow of her back, pooling there.

"It shines like gold against your skin," he murmured, setting his palms over the silken liquid.

She let out a moan of approval as he slid his touch upward, applying just the right amount of pressure. His fingers seemed to trace her ribs, and when he reached the top of her shoulders, he gently worked little circles, looking for the knot that bothered her.

"Feel good?" he asked.

"Mm, yes." She seemed to sink further into the bed as he found the uncomfortable little area of tension. Slowly and patiently, he worked it away.

Isabella concentrated on what he was doing, but she was also very aware of his cock sitting between her buttocks, in the crack. It was both exciting and sensual. She knew she'd soon be impatient for more.

"I wish to take all of your worries away," he said, leaning forward and kissing her neck.

"I am worried about nothing, nothing at all at this moment in time."

"That is good." He curled his fingers over her shoulders, massaging the muscles and tendons there. Then he straightened and swooped down her back, following the vertebrae of her spine. Tapping over each bone, tracing each muscle, every dip and rise.

"That feels so nice," she said, again sighing. "I must rub the oil on you."

"Another time." He spread the oil onto her buttocks.

She tensed, having not expected the oil there. But then he worked up her back to her neck and she once again relaxed.

"You truly have the body of a goddess," he said, moving a little lower so he was straddling her thighs. "One that I am privileged to worship."

"You are emperor. It is your right."

"It is an honor, my love." He paused and again worked the oil onto her buttocks. All over them, in the curve where they met her thighs and around to her hip points. "And I enjoy every moment."

He slipped his fingers down the crease of her buttocks. Slowly. So slowly. As he neared her most private hole, she held her breath. Her toes curled. But he simply slipped his lubricated fingertip over it, lingering for barely a heartbeat before finding her entrance.

"Do you want me as much as I want you?" he murmured.

"Yes. Oh, yes." She tried to part her legs, but he held her trapped.

Not so trapped that he couldn't ease into her, which he did, with two fingers, stretching her deliciously.

A rush of lust burst into her veins and she moaned and arched her spine, pushing back for more. "Charles. My love."

"I told you, we are taking it slow. Enjoy this moment."

Forcing herself to relax and harness her desire, she rocked gently with his soft, penetrating movements. Her own arousal combined with the fragrant oil. Every now and then, little mewls of need escaped her lips.

"You feel amazing," he said, palming her left buttock with his free hand and squeezing. "Every bit of you. I want to know all of you."

"You can." She was getting hot. Her need had been stoked. He was so good at getting her trembling for his cock. "Please...Charles..."

"Tell me what you want."

"You. I want you." She arched her back, tossing her head from one side to the other. "Oh, please, let us join as one."

He tipped forward, his lips hovering over her nape, his breaths blowing hot. "I want you too, so badly, so much. Are you sure you can take it?"

"Yes. I can take everything you want to give me. You know I can."

He didn't answer. Instead, he removed his fingers from inside of her and slipped his body a little lower.

The next thing she knew, his cock was nudging at her cunny. "Oh, yes...that's it." She pushed back, hollowing her spine, and took him the first inch.

He moaned and gripped her hips. "Isabella. Oh..." He pushed in, a determined glide to full depth.

She held her breath and slid one hand between her body and the bed. Quickly, she found her nub and applied pressure.

He groaned, a deep, primitive sound, and hit full depth.

She gasped and clenched around him.

"Oh, my love. This oil." He slid his chest onto her back. "It is a wonderful gift."

And it was. It seemed to bring them even closer. As though their skin were one, each glide a single movement. The smell of rose petals was intense. She'd never pick that flower again and not think of this moment.

"I want you to find pleasure, like this," he said, curling his fingers over her hand. "Let it take you."

"Yes. Yes." She canted her hips and worked her nub. "It's so good like this." It was as though his cock were touching a different place deep inside of her. She'd felt it before, but right now, it was so powerful.

"Are you ready?" he asked.

But he didn't wait for an answer. He pulled almost out then pushed back in, reaching beneath her to palm her right breast as he did so. He set up a fast rhythm that pushed her quickly toward her climax.

Heat pulsed through her. Her belly tightened. Her breaths were hard to catch. A cascade of ecstasy was welling in her pelvis. Still, she worked her nub, grasping each slide of his cock and pushing up to meet him.

Her heart pounded so hard, her pulse echoed in her ears. He was so hard inside her, the oil slick around his cock making it reach what felt like new depths.

"Oh! Oh!" she cried out. "Don't stop."

The bed creaked with each pound and their flesh slapped. Her climax rushed toward her, deep and concentrated. She held her breath for a moment of bliss, then let the pleasure flow from her.

Her toes curled; she fisted the sheets. Her back was hot and trembling against his chest. "Charles!"

"My love." His voice was strained as he stayed with her, pushing her pleasure to new heights.

She squirmed beneath him, harnessing every last delicious, breath-stealing spasm.

Eventually, she slowed and opened her eyes. She stared at the dancing fire.

Charles was still inside her, his body over hers.

"But you..." she managed breathlessly. "You haven't..."

"Shh." He kissed her cheek then sat upright. He was still buried deep.

Her back felt cold without his body heat. "What are—?" He always tried to find his pleasure when she did. He'd said he liked it that way.

"You said you wondered what other things men talk of in the dead of the night when weary from travels."

She didn't answer. He was pouring more oil into the hollow of her back.

"They talk of women," he said. "I only listen, but that suffices."

"You have me curious." A trickle of oil tickled its way to her waist. She swallowed, wondering where Charles was going with this.

"I am not sure if I should tell you." He rubbed the oil into her skin, again onto her buttocks, and then the crack between them.

Another trickle went lower, to her back hole. She tensed.

"But I could show you," he said softly. "Would you like that?"

"I...I don't know."

"You said you trusted me." The tip of his finger traced the oil that had dribbled through her crack. "Was that not true?"

"It is true." And it was. It really was. She did trust him.

"So just relax and let us try this." He ran his finger to her hole. But this time, he didn't move on, he lingered, and then he lingered some more. And then very gently, he rubbed around it, smearing the oil into the tiny wrinkles of skin.

"Oh...Charles, I don't know if..."

"It will be good to be touched here?" He pressed at the center, very gently, and found a little purchase.

She gasped and closed her eyes. The flames still danced in her vision.

"It will be good for both of us. That is what I heard talk of. A man entering a woman here. For pleasure."

Did he mean to...? The thought flew from her mind as he eased into her. A place she'd never thought she'd be touched. The sensation was hot and dark and felt oh-so-sinful. But also, it was exciting and new and sparked her curiosity.

"Ah, my love, you have my cock hardening even further for you."

She was aware of that. He was still inside her cunny.

"Charles, but...what...?" Her internal muscles fluttered around him.

"Rub yourself again, feel everything," he murmured, his fingertip delving deeper. "Ah, yeah...you're going to grip me tightly."

"Oh..." She fretted her nub. It was still swollen and sensitive. "Oh, Charles."

"That's it," he murmured, going deeper inside of her.

She felt so owned by him, so laid open and bare—no part of her wasn't for him.

"Relax," he said. "Relax and just feel, don't think." The finger inside her went deeper, until she could sense his knuckle pressing on her cheeks.

Concentrating, she blew out a breath. A tremble went over her skin, tapping down her spine to her hole.

Suddenly, he pulled his cock from her cunny.

She tensed again. Was he going to plunge his erection into her delicate behind?

"No, stay relaxed, as you were," he said calmly. "I will be gentle. I will not hurt you. I wouldn't hurt you for all the land and power in the world."

She knew he spoke the truth and so managed to relax.

A new stretching in her back hole. The tight ring of muscle being opened further. He'd added another finger, but she stayed relaxed— she didn't fight it. She welcomed it and rubbed her nub a little harder and faster.

"That's so good, my love. Oh, forgive me, but you look so desirable like this." He spread more oil over her buttocks and gently pushed both fingers knuckle-deep. "I am watching it all, seeing this moment of you opening for me."

She groaned and arched her spine. A strange, dense need for more was gripping her.

"Ah, Isabella." He used his fingers on her like he would his cock, in and out, in and out, working her until she was panting.

"Oh…oh…Charles." Sweat peppered her forehead and her belly was tight. Pressure was building in her nub again and a thought for what the explosion would be like with her back hole full crossed her mind.

"Tell me what you want," he commanded. "Tell me."

She was squirming beneath him. "Oh…I want…I want you."

"Where do you want me?" He sounded breathless too, despite being almost still, apart from what he was doing to her with his fingers.

"I…I want you…there."

"Here?" He buried deep, wriggling inside her. "Do you want my cock here?"

She groaned, deep and guttural, a primitive sound that came from low in her chest. "Oh…"

"I'll take that as a yes."

He pulled his fingers out. Her hole clamped shut and she moaned at the loss.

He was over her, his broad, hot chest on her back, his lips by her ear. "Keep touching yourself. Don't stop, not even for a moment."

"I…I won't." Her wrist ached, but still, she worked herself. It felt too good not to.

"And relax again," he said. "My cock is slick with oil. It won't hurt when it goes in."

"But what if…" She twisted to look at him. "Isn't this a terrible sin?"

"No, my love. We are simply man and wife finding pleasure."

"But…are you sure? Isn't it sod—"

He kissed her cheek. "I am emperor. This is not a sin. I know this is so."

She didn't have any more argument in her, for his cock was there—wide, heated, slick, and demanding.

It took a lot of willpower to keep herself pliant and not panic. How would he fit...there?

"Oh, my love." Again, he weaved his fingers with hers, their joined hands pressing against the bed.

Then slowly, carefully, gently, he curled his hips and delicately pushed into her. His width opened her hole, stretching the flesh around his cock tip until it felt like it could stretch no more.

She gasped at the nip of pain. But it was over in a second and then he was sliding into her. An easy glide despite his size that filled her with a glorious heavy weight that went so deep.

"Oh, good Lord above." He moaned as his body curled into hers and he buried as deep as he could go. "You're so soft in here, and warm...it's...incredible."

"Charles."

"Am I hurting you?" There was a sudden note of anxiety in his voice.

"No. No..." She was breathing shallowly. "Oh, but I want to...I want to find pleasure like this...both of us."

"We will." He released her hand and slipped his between her body and the bed. "Let me, let me touch you." He found her nub and set up a gentle, circular motion—one he knew drove her wild with need.

She groaned and her back hole tightened around the root of his cock.

He snapped in a breath. "I won't last long." He gasped. "Find pleasure when you can."

"I can... It's not far off...I can... Oh..." She screwed up her eyes. The illicit sensations in her behind were building up to a crescendo and her nub was getting ready to release its tension. "Oh, please. Yes. Like that...don't stop. Don't stop. Charles. Don't...stop."

He was barely moving inside of her, the sweetest little thrusts. But that was enough and within a few seconds, she was holding her breath and preparing for the fall into bliss.

"Urgh!" He grunted loudly. His next thrust was a little more powerful, and then his cock was pulsing inside her. She could feel every wave of pleasure up his shaft.

Her own climax claimed her. Ecstasy spread from her nub to her cunny to her back hole. She clenched around his cock, eliciting another deep grunt from him. It was as if her body were possessed for a few sweet moments and she spasmed and twitched as the pleasure flowed through her veins.

Their moans of satisfaction combined. Charles indulged in a few more tender rides into her, deep, deeper still. She welcomed it. She loved it all. Who would have thought?

"My love...are you well after that?" he asked, easing up on her nub.

"Yes. Yes...oh, yes."

He lifted his weight a fraction. "You are so giving, so wonderful, so beautiful. I love you so much."

"As I love you." She was breathing hard, and her body was still being ravaged by sporadic little muscle spasms.

He brushed her hair from her cheek and kissed her. "Will you let me take you this way again?"

"Yes...with the oil, it is incredible."

"I am so glad it is for you too," he whispered. "I'd felt confident it would be for me, but I did not want pleasure alone. I always want you to find pleasure, no matter what we do."

She didn't answer as he pulled from her and flopped onto his back.

Quickly, she curled onto her side, and he pulled her close into the crook of his arm. Their warm flesh was slick and glossy with sweat.

"Do you need a blanket?" he asked.

"No, you have heated me considerably, husband of mine."

He smiled and kissed the top of her head, holding her a little tighter.

"Now I am even more curious as to what else the men talk of," she said, tracing a circle around his right nipple then moving to do the same to the left.

"Many dull things, if truth be told." His breathing was returning to normal. "But sometimes, late at night around the fire, they talk of women and pleasure."

"And you just listen? Nothing more?"

"Naturally, for I would not share a single detail of my wife, the empress. But as we have just found out, it pays to use one's ears."

She laughed softly. "They do not ask you?"

"They would not dare."

She paused, then, "May I ask you something?"

"Of course."

She propped herself onto her elbow and studied his handsome face. His cheeks were a little flushed and his eyes had a look of too much wine, though she knew that wasn't the case.

He tucked a strand of hair behind her ear. "What is it you want to ask?"

"You are Holy Roman Emperor."

"Last time I checked." He smiled.

"So if one day when you stand before God and the devil himself…"

"Go on?" A slight frown marred his brow and he rested his palm on her bare shoulder.

"What one thing would you sell your soul to the devil for?"

"What one thing?" he repeated.

"Yes. If you were to give up an eternity in heaven for one thing, what would it be?"

"That is an easy question."

"Really? Even as the King of Christendom?" She was surprised.

"Yes, my love. For I would give up everything, my soul included, to have a lifetime with you. A full and long life, that ends in wrinkles on our saggy skin, gray in our hair, and grandchildren at our feet."

"Grandchildren at our feet." She brushed her lips over his. "Wouldn't that be a thing? For our family to go on for generation after generation ruling Spain, ruling Europe? Spreading the holy word of God?"

"Yes, Isabella, wouldn't that be a truly remarkable achievement?" He pulled her close and set a full kiss on her lips as he wound his legs with hers.

The log on the fire popped, a tawny owl hooted outside, and in the distance, a dog barked. Isabella knew happiness was a rare thing. It must be enjoyed when chanced upon. Savored. Appreciated. Treasured. And the happiness she felt right now was one that few mortals ever got to experience.

It was the happiness of an empress being embraced by her emperor and the sense that the rest of the world and all of its problems had faded into the distance.

Only time would tell what was to become of their family. The history books would know it...but they hadn't been written yet.

THE END

Book Club Questions

Embraced by the Emperor

1. Do you feel that Charles believes himself to be a god-like figure? Perhaps someone who is closer to God than his people, as though he has a direct line to speak to Him? And if so, does this make you like him less or is that just how emperors behave?

2. What words would you use to describe Isabella and does she change throughout the book?

3. How did the books' titles and the series title fit the trilogy? If you could rename anything, what would it be?

4. How did HAWK CASTLE impact you? Do you think you'll remember it in a few years?

5. Are there any lingering questions from the book you're still thinking about?

6. Did you Google anything while reading? For example, the attack Charles and Isabella's young son, Philip, went onto initiate... can you guess?

7. Did you Google the real-life characters when you'd finished reading to find out their ultimate fates? And if so, how well did the books do to finish on a happily ever after?

8. Which character in the series did you relate to the most?

9. If you had the chance to become one character in HAWK CAS-TLE, who would it be?

10. If *Embraced by the Emperor* were a Netflix series, who would play Charles and Isabella?

Character Interview

Embraced by the Emperor

Hop on over to Lily Harlem's website to enjoy an exclusive interview with Charles and Isabella.

www.lilyharlem.com/charles-and-isabella.html

Suggested Playlist for

Embraced by the Emperor

"The Crown Main Title" – Hans Zimmer

"When I Fall in Love (feat. Chris Botti)" – Renee Olstead, Chris Botti

"Angel By The Wings" – Sia

"Emperor's New Clothes" – PANIC! At The Disco

"I Do" – Colbie Caillat

"Naked as We Came" – Iron & Wine

"Falling" – Julee Cruise

"Slow Down" – Kyle Church

"For the Glory" – All Good Things

"Say Something" – A Great Big World

"exile (feat. Bon Iver)" – Taylor Swift, Bon Iver

"Every Night" – Imagine Dragons

"Keep Me From The Cold" – Curtis Stigers

"I Found" – Amber Run

"Anchor" – Novo Amor

"Wings" – Birdy

"Circles (based on Ludovico Einaudi's "Experience")" – Greta Svabo
Bech, Ludovico Einaudi

About the Author

Based in the UK, Lily Harlem is an award-winning, *USA Today* bestselling author of sexy romance. She's a complete floozy when it comes to genres and pairings, writing saucy historical, heterosexual kink, gay paranormal, and everything in between. She's also very partial to a happily ever after.

If you're a Kindle Unlimited subscriber, you can read many of her books for free, including several complete series, and if you love sporty romances, get the first novel in her popular HOT ICE series when you sign up for her newsletter.

One thing you can be sure of, whatever book you pick up by Ms. Harlem, is it will be wildly romantic and deliciously sexy. Enjoy!

Website: www.lilyharlem.com
Amazon Author Page: author.to/LilyHarlem
Lily's Reader Group: facebook.com/groups/188731774881774

Find your next book boyfriend…
Male/Female
Male/Male
Historical Romance
Paranormal
Menage a Trois
Reverse Harem
Audio Books

For more deliciously steamy historical romance, including a plethora of stern Highlanders, dashing dukes, and kinky Vikings, visit Lily's website.

Made in the USA
Coppell, TX
11 November 2024

39514079R00125